The
PURPOSE
BENEATH

CODY K. MILLS

ISBN 978-1-0980-5751-0 (paperback)
ISBN 978-1-0980-6053-4 (hardcover)
ISBN 978-1-0980-5752-7 (digital)

Christian Faith Publishing, Inc.
832 Park Avenue
Meadville, PA 16335
www.christianfaithpublishing.com

Printed in the United States of America

For my wife and children

FOREWORD

The little town of East Lynn had been riding the coal boom for many years. A fire had destroyed most of the town in 1955, and with the mine's spark fizzling out, most of its inhabitants were left looking for work. In the early 1960s, a flood ravaged the town of East Lynn and eventually led the US Army Corps of Engineers to build what is now East Lynn Lake. When the lake was flooded, it took the small community of Stiltner and submerged a piece of history that will forever lie in the depths of the muddy waters. Like most coal towns in West Virginia, once the coal ran out, so did the people. The mid-1960s was a trying time not only for this small town but for America itself. We were faced with the Civil Rights Movement on top of Vietnam and the Watergate scandal. Many young men were called to fight in a political war, and these men were looked down upon by part of our society. Whatever the political motive or occurrences within our United States, each man had a story. For the men who went to war, it was an unpleasant one, more often than not, but also one of courage and selflessness. These stories show time and time again that heroes come in many different shapes, sizes, colors, and heritages, and God seems to use people to achieve his plan no matter their circumstances. This story in particular highlights the life of struggle for a small mining town in West Virginia and its citizens during this time. This story is based on actual events.

PROLOGUE

"Hey! Get up!"

Thomas's vision cleared to see Doc's gnarled face screaming just inches from his. There were tiny pieces of shrapnel sticking in his cheekbone, and blood was oozing out of a gash just over his left eye.

"Get up, Tom! We're going to get killed! We're sitting ducks!"

Thomas got up off the jungle canopy. He had a deafening ring in his ear, and he couldn't catch his balance. His vision in his right eye was gone. He reached up to feel for his eyeball. His hand was shaking uncontrollably. He couldn't feel his fingers. Thomas looked down at his hand to see that three of his fingers had been blown off.

"Doc, my hand…" Thomas looked at Doc as bullets zipped by his ears, spraying the trees above and beside him.

"I know, buddy. Don't worry about your hand. It'll be all right!" Doc screamed as dirt spat up all around the three of them. "We're gonna get killed if we don't get out of here!"

Thomas consciousness came back within him as a bullet grazed the top of his shoulder. It shocked Thomas and sent him back to the ground. He got to his knees and crawled over to Tray. Thomas grabbed Tray's shoulders and dragged him behind a tree. Tray's legs were useless. He had taken multiple gunshots to his knees and thighs, and blood was spurting out of one hole every time his heart took a beat. Thomas looked at him with sweat and blood dripping off his chin.

"Tray, this is going to hurt real bad, buddy. Look at me!"

"Thomas, am I going to die?" Tray asked with what little breath he could squeeze out.

"No, buddy, this is just a minor wound. You are going to be okay."

Doc looked at Thomas from a few feet away. Thomas looked at Doc and turned his eyes back to Tray. He was very pale, and his eyes started to roll back in his head. Thomas sank his fingers into the bullet hole and fished around for the artery in Tray's leg. His fingers slipped on and off until, finally, Thomas was able to pinch off the spurting artery. Tray had taken his bandana off and was screaming into the cloth as Doc finally was able to make his way to them. Thomas looked at Doc as he picked up a handful of mud and stuffed it into the gaping hole on Tray's leg.

"There's no time, Thomas. We've got to get out—"

Doc's sentence was cut short as a bullet passed through his cheekbone.

CHAPTER 1

Darkness

Three years earlier…

Thomas sat in darkness and watched as the flame danced on the tip of the candle's wick. He squinted a bit and wondered at the personality of the flame moving slightly when a draft passed from beneath the crack in the log cabin's front door. The flame seemed so unfamiliar to him. Its warmth and light lit the room dimly. Thomas wondered what it would take to spark the flame that had once danced inside of him. Thomas took a deep breath and blew out the candle. Darkness immediately consumed the room, and Thomas at once felt more comfortable.

Thomas was just a young boy when his mother had her accident. He couldn't remember much about the days when she was a healthy woman. She was always bedridden. He could remember his father crying at night in the living room where he thought no one would hear in the first few years after the accident. At first, Thomas would cry into his pillow when he heard his father weeping at the foot of his mother's bed; but after years of exposure, the pain began to numb him. Thomas grew older, and his mother eventually grew into an unresponsive and empty vessel. She stopped eating and drinking, and her weight rapidly decreased. His father aged more quickly than the other men in town due to the stress, and his appearance made him seem like a ghost. His eyes were dark as night and sank into his skull, and the wrinkles seemed to map out the long years he had suffered through, telling a story of his heartache and pain. His beard matted around his mouth from the small meals he would eat. The odor that seemed to fill the house of liquor mixed with body odor had become a permanent stench, and Thomas suffered dearly. His classmates always teased him and called him worthless. They gave him nicknames like "dirtbag Tom" and "mutt." Thomas didn't have many friends. He was a lonely kid. His father and mother were his only family besides his uncle, who lived over in Kentucky, and Thomas had just seen him a few times.

Thomas slowly grew into a young man and eventually dropped out of school in order to help his father pay his mother's medical bills. Thomas dreaded going to work in the mines. He hated the darkness and the depth, and somehow he felt the darkness of the mines crept into his soul. After years of his internal turmoil, the darkness seemed more like a part of him than the light. Although he hated the mines, he could at least escape his drunkard of a father at work.

As Thomas tightened the laces on his boots, he imagined that his insides must look like the rock he chiseled out of the inside of the mountains he seemed to live in. He was cold, dark, and dusty just as the hollowed-out ground he dug into. It was something he felt he could never escape, inside or outside of work, and it was a pain going and working a twelve-hour shift six days a week. Thomas was the youngest man working in the mines. He would look at the men who surrounded him, most of whom were in their forties or fifties, and saw how broken down this decrepit hole had made them, but this was all they had. This job provided for their families, and some had traveled here from miles or were born into this life. Thomas felt that he would live this same life. There was no escaping the chains that came with living in the sleepy town that caged him. While all Thomas's classmates were successful in their studies and always talked about their plans of attending college once they graduated, Thomas sat and soaked in the reality of the inescapable truth. His plan and path seemed to be chosen for him. Life had become a black fog and had suffocated any hopes or aspirations he had in life.

Thomas followed in his father's footsteps when it came to alcohol. It seemed to numb the pain temporarily, but always brought him down once the drunkenness faded away. He was more or less a punching bag around town. His former classmates took advantage of Thomas being weak and outnumbered. For a seventeen-year-old boy, it was not an easy task providing for a family and barely making enough to pay for a small meal each day due to his mother's medical bills. He wasn't frail, but he was weak because the labor took the life out of him. The local bullies seemed to be aware of this. He made a conscious effort to go on the outskirts of town on his way home from work so he wouldn't get beat up. Everyday life was a battle for him.

Thomas would be eighteen years old soon. His classmates would graduate and go to college. Some would go straight to work for their fathers' businesses. A lot of kids around town took their daddies' handouts. Most kids would be excited to be turning eighteen years old because they would now be independent. Thomas had been on his own basically since he was thirteen years old. He knew how tough life was, and the chance of him escaping the darkness that he was consumed in was, well, slim to none. He knew what the future held for him. He was to live and die in this sleepy mining town, and every day from here on out would be difficult for him. That was a realization that he had grown to accept years ago.

As Thomas worked through his shift, each shovel full of coal seemed to get heavier and heavier. The shovel became an extension of his arms. Finally, each day, his shift would end, and the mine shaft elevator would slowly elevate him back into the world above. There was only one thing that took the ache out of his body, and Thomas had grown to enjoy the soothing and relaxation he found in the bottom of a whiskey bottle.

A few shots sounded better than a fluffy bed with clean sheets after shoveling the rock out of that mountainside. But today had been especially hard because the temperature had dropped to five degrees, and a foot of snow fell. It was just what Thomas had hoped for: a butt whipping both mentally and physically. That was a tough few miles to walk home in and an even tougher twelve-hour shift to work through due to the fact he couldn't afford a new coat, and the one he had was full of holes from crawling through the mines. The cold grasped Thomas's body like a python and squeezed the life out of him. Every move was an awaiting muscle spasm. Maybe today he would have a few more drinks than usual if he could afford it.

Thomas stopped at the local grocery to buy himself a pack of cigarettes. Cigarettes helped him relax, and since black lung disease was nearly unavoidable, he figured it wouldn't hurt him more than the devil dust he breathed in on a daily basis. Thomas always like going into the store after work because he always caught the news on the one television he could watch for a short period of time. It was December 1964. President Kennedy had been assassinated a year earlier, and President Johnson was talking on the television this evening. Thomas lit the tip of his cigarette and tossed the match over his shoulder—sweet nicotine. Thomas exhaled, and the white smoke fogged the glass. It seemed like the past few weeks on the news, all President Johnson and the rest of the newspeople wanted to talk about was Vietnam. Thomas didn't think much about it. Truthfully, who the hell cared about what was going on half a world away? He couldn't relate to a fight that was happening halfway around the world, and all he knew was East Lynn, West Virginia. Thomas decided that he would skip the news broadcast and head to the bar. There was an icy shot glass waiting on him. Thomas shuffled his feet to the very thought of that beautiful bourbon burning down his throat. He was miserable and needed an escape as quickly as possible. His joints felt like rusty hinges, and his back felt like someone took a club to it.

Thomas lost track of the whiskey rounds after ten. It was a well-known fact that he could drink a middle-aged man under the table. His grandfather had been in the Navy, and Thomas always thought his tolerance level came from genetics. Soon he shed his jacket and was thinking about his miserable life. He felt hatred toward his father. Thomas resented having to break his back for his mother while his father spent all the money on alcohol. He always wondered how a grown man could abandon his only son and give his life up to the bottle. Thomas slid down the corner in the bar to the floor. "Damn that man." Thomas's eyelids weighed heavily, then sank closed.

When Thomas awoke, he was lying on the floor. He tried to regain his clarity of vision by wiping his eyes, but it seemed his brain was clouding his vision instead of the sleep he just awoke from. His head was aching, and his body felt cold. But all the while, he did recognize the floor was a velvet color. Thomas tried to think where he might be, but it hurt to try and process a thought. The last time he had seen a floor this color was when he was a child and his aunt had brought him to church. He must be in the church house.

Thomas slowly raised his body off the floor and looked around. There, standing, was Mr. Krauss.

"I found you lying outside of the bar in the snow. I picked you up and carried you here so you wouldn't freeze to death," Mr. Krauss explained to Thomas.

"Thanks for the help," Thomas said.

"Well, by the look of it, you not only needed my help, but you need God's help, Thomas. I've seen you around town. You seem like you're lost, son."

"Ah, preacher, don't worry about my soul. You ought to worry about the people with a future and a soul left to save. I wasn't aware that anyone cared I was hurting, considering I've been abused for as long as I can remember," Thomas replied. "I think I'll be going now, preacher-man." Thomas staggered toward the door.

"Hold on now, son. You think that God only wants the worthy?"

Thomas thought about Mr. Krauss's question. "Yes, sir. God is for the worthy, and I, sir, am the son of a drunkard and have a lot of the devil in me." Thomas wiped the slobber from his lips. His feet tingled, and his head felt lopsided.

"Thomas, did you know Jesus was hated by not only the pharisees but the people as well? Not all of them, but Jesus was an outcast. He conversed with prostitutes and the possessed. Jesus himself was shunned by mostly everyone around him that thought they were worthy, even more so than the *Son of God*," Mr. Krauss explained to Thomas.

Thomas thought about it for a minute, but he didn't understand Mr. Krauss's point. "I'm not following you, preacher-man."

"Thomas, my point is, we are all unworthy in the eyes of God, but because Jesus sacrificed his life to save us from our sins, we can all enter the kingdom of heaven if we repent of our sins and accept Jesus as our Savior. It doesn't matter who our parents are, what we have done in the past, or what color or nationality we are. God even loves prostitutes, gay people, and everyone else society deems the bottom of the barrel. It doesn't mean they are right in what they do, but God still loves them. We are all his children."

"Well, preacher, I'll give this all a thought once I get this whiskey out of my system," Thomas said as he tripped out the front entrance of the church house.

Thomas headed home still feeling like he could have possibly been hit by a truck the following night. He remembered it was Sunday morning. He walked for nearly forty minutes. He was freezing cold and dehydrated from the whiskey, but another shot sure would taste good on his lips right about now. His legs could barely make it through the thick snow, and each step was more miserable than the last one. Finally, he made it to his house up the mountain.

Thomas leaned over and puked. He finally managed to pull both boots off. His father hated when he got his socks wet, and Thomas knew from the whip of his father's belt not to walk inside with his wet boots. Thomas had been wearing the same pair of socks for two weeks now. His feet smelled putrid and burned like he had been tap-dancing with the devil. Athlete's foot had set in long ago. He soaked his feet in water that he set on his woodburning stove for a few minutes and poured salt he stole from the market. He got his shoes off and walked inside. There, his father was lying on the floor, weeping. This was a normal sight, so Thomas headed to his room to bury himself in his bed.

"Your mother is dead, Thomas. She died last night while you were slobbering drunk at the bar. I know you were there because Father Krauss sent word that he dragged you out of the snow," Thomas's father said, weeping every word.

Thomas just looked at his father in confusion. "Ma is dead?" Tears came to Thomas's eyes. He didn't know his mother well, but he heard stories from around town how good of a woman she was.

She was a churchgoer, and so was his father, until a year or so after the accident.

Thomas had had enough of this. He had enough of this pain. He had enough of his father's weeping, and as disgusted he was, he couldn't help but feel that he was the same as his father. He was just a drunkard. His life had become meaningless. He had enough of the mines. He had enough of the darkness and the callouses that had formed from thrusting a shovel for the past five years every day for sixteen hours a day. He had enough of life. He must end this torment. So Thomas rushed out of the house barefoot, cold, and miserable. He rushed down the mountainside and headed for the railroad bridge. This was it for Thomas. He was going to end this pain, whatever way he could, and the fastest was way to jump off the bridge into the icy depths of the creek. He was already in a cold, dark place. The depths of the water seemed like a perfect dwelling place for his soul to rest.

CHAPTER 2

Divine Intervention

Thomas reached the bridge. His feet had become numb, and his lungs had filled with fluid. It was freezing outside. He ran onto the bridge and looked down. There was no stopping him. He was done. He took a deep breath, and time seemed to stand still as one foot slipped off the metal of the rail track. As he sat there looking at the rushing water, he wondered why God had made his life so difficult. While other young adults were going to the grocery store and having a soda or playing baseball, Thomas was dealing with the pain of his family or working in the depths of hell.

"I'm finished with this life. God, I don't know if you're up there, but if you are, you did this to me. It's your fault I'm doing this." He lifted his second foot, and just as his toes began to leave the metal, he heard a voice yell, "Stop, Thomas!"

Thomas regained his balance and looked to his right. Nobody was there. Thomas looked to his left. Nobody was there either. Who had yelled at him? Who had stopped him from jumping? Thomas fell backward, and his eyes began to tear up. How could life get so bad, and how could he put up with more torture? Who had told him to stop? Was it God? Did God hate him so much that he wouldn't even let him die in peace?

"Thomas, what are you doing out here barefoot?" Thomas heard someone ask from beneath him.

It was Emily Krauss. Emily was a beautiful girl. She was olive-skinned with rosy cheeks and bright-green eyes with jet-black hair. She was a quiet girl and didn't talk much, but her eyes compensated for what her mouth didn't deliver. She almost seemed self-conscious, as if she didn't know how beautiful she was. She was very well put together and very voluptuous in her hips and chest. Maybe it had been because her father was a preacher and taught her to be humble. Either way, she never seemed to be courted by any boys, and she mainly kept to herself.

"Did you hear me, Thomas? You'll get sick from walking around out here with no shoes on! Come with me, and I will get you something warm to eat and drink."

Thomas was taken aback. He just wanted to cry, but his pride wouldn't let him. He wanted to say no, but it seemed Emily's look of insistence wouldn't let him.

"You're a real bright crayon, aren't you, Thomas Bailey?" Emily asked.

Thomas didn't reply. Actually, he didn't know what to say. What could he say? Emily was so gorgeous she almost looked angelic—and Thomas did all he could to keep his eyes off Emily's…figure. "Uh, well, no," Thomas replied. He decided it was best if he just looked at the ground. That way, she wouldn't rethink her offer.

"You look like you just met the death angel, Thomas. Are you okay? Are you sick?" Emily asked.

"No, I just…I lost my mother." Thomas looked at the ground. His feet were blue.

"Oh, Thomas, are you okay?" she asked as she brought him in her arms.

"Yes," Thomas replied.

"I'm so sorry, Thomas. If there is any way I can help, just let me know."

Emily's hair felt like the feather from an angel's wing tickling his cheek, and she smelled like a freshly cut spring rose. He almost felt a sense of comfort. It made Thomas uncomfortable. He didn't know what comfort felt like.

"I've got to be going. I've got to go pick up some things from the grocery store for my father," he lied.

"Okay, Thomas, but if you ever change your mind, you know where I spend most of my time," Emily said as she nodded toward the church house. "Oh, and you had better put on some shoes before you catch pneumonia," she added as Thomas started off toward his father's cabin.

As Thomas ran back up the hill, he wondered, how could a woman of Emily's stature care about the feelings of a worthless individual like himself? Thomas shook his head. *Get your mind right, Thomas.* Thomas was a young man, after all. Even in his pain, he couldn't help but feel attraction toward Emily.

Thomas reached home and ran up the steps into the old cabin he called home. It had been in his family for a couple generations. His grandfather had built it when he was a younger man. A sudden panic swept over Thomas as the realization his mother was dead came back to his attention.

"Hey, Dad, I'm sorry for running off," Thomas said with tears starting to run down his cheeks. He felt guilty for leaving his father so abruptly.

Thomas had not known his mother too well. She lay in bed most of the time and stared blankly at the ceiling most days, or she slept. Her brain injuries sustained in the accident had left her empty. His father never gave up hope, but after the accident, Thomas's father lost all faith in the God in whom he had once believed so firmly. His whole life revolved around his wife. Thomas's grandfather was abusive to his father, and when he had met Thomas's mother, she set him free from the bondage Mr. Bailey had felt his whole life. She brought him in the church where he felt like he had a family. The years of losing the person he loved so dearly had sucked the life right out of him. Thomas had begun to feel as though his mother were just a burden, and this made Thomas feel guilty at times, but he still loved his mother even though he truly didn't know her.

As Thomas sat down, he noticed his father's bedroom door was open. Thomas sat down and put his feet in some warm water. After a couple minutes, the feeling started to return to his feet. "Hey, Dad."

Thomas didn't hear a reply. His father must be passed out drunk. Thomas got up and dried his feet off. He emptied out the water from the tub off the front of his porch and sat the tub down on the floor. Thomas was tired, so he headed back to his room, which was adjacent to his father's. He opened his door and turned to shut it behind him when he noticed his father's arm lying on the ground, peeking out from behind his own door. Thomas walked over to the door and squeezed his way into the room. There lay his father.

"Dad?" Thomas nudged his father's shoulder with his foot. He didn't respond. "Hey, wake up." Thomas nudged him again on the head. He didn't move. He was cold as ice. A feeling of panic swept over Thomas. "Hey!" Thomas fell on his knees and shook his father. He still was unresponsive. Thomas began to cry. He put his ear down to his father's nose. He couldn't hear anything. Thomas began to weep. He fell upon his father and cried upon his chest. Thomas knew he was dead. He didn't hear his father's heart beating. He looked up and noticed his father was holding a picture of his mother and father in one hand and a whiskey bottle in the other. His father had drunk himself to death trying to numb his pain. Thomas immediately ran down into town to fetch help, but it was too late.

In the following months, Thomas struggled with suicidal thoughts. It didn't help that he spent most of his paychecks to buy alcohol. He searched for any way to relieve the pain and figured if he didn't drink himself to death soon, that bridge was looking more and more like the answer to his problems. He struggled at work, and he showed up drunk. His foreman had been a good friend of his father's, so he told Thomas it was better to take a few weeks off rather than lose his job. He let him finish his shift and then put him on a leave of absence until he could straighten up his act. Thomas had no such plans. Alcohol was an escape. Although it was temporary, it was all he had. Thomas had been drinking so heavily he nearly forgot it was almost Christmas.

After his last shift, he decided that he was going to skip the bar and buy a bottle. It was Christmas, and as much as he loved whiskey, he felt the need to go and see some of the lights rather than the floor of the bathroom in the bar. Thomas usually avoided going into the middle of town because either he was slobbering drunk and could be arrested for public intoxication or feared being beaten and pelted with rocks by the local bullies. Since it was Christmas and in the middle of night, he figured he would be safe from either one. So Thomas grabbed his coffee mug, filled it with whiskey, and headed down the mountainside toward town.

Once Thomas reached town, he headed toward the city hall and the courthouse. Most of the lights on display were close to the courthouse, being as most of the politicians lived nearby, and they had the money to afford Christmas lights. Thomas reached town hall, and there the lights shone beautifully. Red and green and white lights dazzled in the white ocean of snow that fell and blanketed the ground. The lights almost made Thomas feel warm, just not as warm as Emily's hug did. Thomas admired the lights for a few minutes and started to get cold, so he headed back down the street toward his house. He had nearly reached the end of town and was passing the church when he noticed a display of the nativity scene glowing in the pitch-black.

Thomas stopped and looked. He wondered what Joseph had felt like being cast out of the inn and having to tell his wife she must give birth out where the animals ate. Thomas remembered his aunt's teachings from when he was younger. He went to church with his aunt until he had to go to the mines to work. Thomas liked church, but he had become bitter at the thought that God had let him slip into such a miserable state. He questioned why God had made his mother sick and his dad so hopeless. Thomas thought hard about his life and wondered what he would do with himself. He didn't have to work in the mines, but he had no education and no future outside of this town.

Thomas's thoughts were abruptly ended by the thud of something smashing into the side of his face. The blow knocked Thomas to the ground. Pain filled his head, and he could feel blood trickling down his cheek to his chin and pooling on the ground. Thomas looked up. It was who he feared it would be: it was Zack Lindsey and his buddies. The boys from school had decided to stay out late, and Thomas was going to pay for it.

"What are you doing in town, mutt butt? You look like you need a shower. Tell you what, I'll do you a favor. Boys, grab Thomas and give him a bath."

The boys gathered around Thomas and kicked and punched him until he quit fighting. They carried him over to a puddle in the street and put him facedown. One by one, they pressed his face under the water for a few seconds and then let him up to breathe so he wouldn't drown. They left Thomas lying there. He wasn't near death, but he was in great pain. The blow had given Thomas a minor concussion, and the boys kicking him had broken a couple ribs and Thomas's ankle. Thomas wanted to just lie there until someone came, but if he did that, he would freeze to death. He raised his head to look and see if there were somewhere he could crawl to escape the cold. Everything was locked up, and there were no homes within a couple blocks. He tried to get up, but his broken ankle left him with one leg, and his other leg was so badly bruised and cut from the beating he couldn't walk. Thomas knew he might die on this night. He had wanted to die earlier, but now that this choice was made for him, he didn't want to. He wanted it to be his own choice if he died, not by someone else's hands.

Thomas was at his lowest point. Things couldn't get much worse. He was freezing, wet, and he suspected his ankle was broken. His stomach was flip-flopping, and his equilibrium was off. He hated the world and everything about it. In his hatred and pain, Thomas rolled on his back and stared at the sky. It was a clear night, and the stars were shining brightly. A shooting star crossed the sky above Thomas. He sat up and watched the star pass out of sight beyond the mountains ahead. Thomas looked down from the star, and ahead of him was the nativity scene. Its lights shone brightly in the dark, and the beautiful porcelain figurines stood softly in the snowy blanket of the night. Its hay tinted the scene with a golden glow. Thomas picked up a rock and hurled it toward the porcelain figurines. He struggled but managed to rise to his feet and hobbled over to the church. He sat down on the steps leading up to the stained glass doors.

"I should have just gone to the bar." Thomas wiped the blood from his nose and spat the rest onto the gravel. "What do I do now,

God?" Thomas looked up in the sky. "If you're up there, tell me what am I supposed to do?" Thomas yelled. "You have punished me my entire life! I know you're up there, so answer me! I've got nothing!"

Thomas, in his emotional outrage, fell backward on the steps. He lay there and watched his breath in the frigid night air.

"You know, it's awfully cold to be sleeping outside, Mr. Bailey."

Thomas sat up abruptly. Mr. Krauss was standing in the church's doorway. He shut the door and stepped down to sit beside Thomas. Thomas quickly tried to wipe the tears and the rest of the blood from his face.

"You know, something I've always found fascinating about God is how he communicates to us. The Bible says God works in myste-rious ways, Thomas."

"Ha!" Thomas laughed. "Mysterious—indeed, sir."

"You know, your father once told me the only thing that saved his life was your mother."

Thomas looked at Mr. Krauss. "Well, looks to me it was the thing that ruined his also."

There were a few seconds of silence.

"Your father was a good man once."

Thomas smirked and shook his head. "The only thing my father ever did well was tan my behind with his leather belt."

"Did your father ever tell you how we first met, Thomas?" Mr. Krauss asked.

Thomas shook his head.

Mr. Krauss twiddled his fingers and rubbed his hands together. "My mother was a good, wholesome woman, Thomas. She did all she could for me and my brothers. She would sew and make quilts all year long to earn some money. At the end of the year, she would go sell the quilts she made so she could buy me and my brothers gifts for Christmas. We always got fresh oranges and peppermint sticks." Mr. Krauss stopped his story and continued to rub his palms together.

Thomas's attention was now on Mr. Krauss, and he could feel his tension. "So what's that got to do with my dad?"

Mr. Krauss stared at the ground.

"One day my mother was in town buying our Christmas gifts. She had waited later than usual to go. The sun had already set, and most people had turned in for the night. It was busy, and a lot of people were just passing through because of the holiday season. There were a lot of drifters looking for charity that came in on the railcars. She had just paid for our gifts and headed back toward our house when she was stopped by some drifters in the alleyway beside the bar. They took her in the back alley and hurt her."

Mr. Krauss voice cracked. Thomas looked quietly at Mr. Krauss. His eyes began to fill with tears. "Your father was also at the store buying your mother some flour. He headed out soon after my mother had from the store when he passed by the alley and heard my mother struggling. He stopped to see what was going on and tried to help my mother. Of course, he was outnumbered, and the men beat him to a bloody pulp, but your father was a tough man. He was as stubborn as you are. He never quit. He just kept getting right back up and took a beating each time he got to his feet. My mother was able to crawl away. It took her hours, but my father came looking for her after it got late. She told my father about your daddy coming to help her and nearly getting beat to death trying to save her."

A lump had developed in Thomas's throat. He had never thought of his father in the light that Mr. Krauss described him.

"The tragic aspect of this story is that your mother eventually got worried about your father. Your mother was very strong-willed, Thomas. *Fearless* is a good word to describe her. Her personality was powerful, and she set out looking for your father. There was a bad storm that night that had blown in. It was raining a downpour. As she was heading off the mountain, a lightning bolt struck a tree near your mother. It spooked the horse she was riding and bucked her off. When she fell, her head struck a boulder, and she never recovered. It did something to her mind after she hit that boulder. That is how she became sick and was bedridden all those years before she passed. Your father took it hard. The first few years, he didn't give up hope. He practically stayed either in church or beside your mother. He believed with all his heart she would snap out of it. When nothing changed, his hope faded. He blamed himself. After a while he quit coming in the church and attending services and took a different route. He turned to alcohol to help his suffering."

"So what was his excuse for turning his back on me?" Thomas interrupted.

Father Krauss became silent. He thought for a minute and then looked at Thomas. "I see the good in you, Thomas, just as I did in your mother and, at one point, also in your father. Truthfully, I can't answer that question. Maybe your father's bitterness hardened his heart, and once that happened, his entire life became too bitter a thing for him to see the good things he still had. Whatever the reason, it was no excuse to neglect you the way he did. If you want answers, I'm not the person to give them. There is, however, someone who can most likely give you those answers, Thomas. If answers are what you are after, all you have to do is listen. Sometimes the door to a man's soul is being knocked on, but he's just not listening closely enough, or maybe he's just not listening at all."

Mr. Krauss got to his feet and headed back up the steps to the church's entrance. He stopped as he went through the door and turned to Thomas. "God will tell you everything you need to know, Thomas. You just have to get rid of your own bitterness to hear him. Why don't you come over tomorrow to our home for dinner? It's probably been a while since you've had a good meal."

Thomas sat quietly, thinking about everything Mr. Krauss had said.

"Well, just think about it. Mrs. Krauss will have dinner ready by six. I hope you decide to come. My daughter seems to think highly of you, so I want to get to know you a little better also."

Thomas's attention was directed to the offer as soon as the last few words Mr. Krauss said sank in. Mr. Krauss shut the door, and Thomas was left to sit and ponder with all his emotions running wildly within.

The next day, Thomas woke up after just sleeping for a few hours. He tossed and turned all night thinking about his feelings toward his father and the offer Mr. Krauss had mentioned. There were a lot of things on his mind he just couldn't absorb. He was also afraid to go to dinner at the Krausses' home because he had no decent clothes. As he sat contemplating whether or not to go, he remembered his father's old church clothes. It had been years since his father had worn them, but even though they were old and out of style, they were at least presentable at a dinner table. Thomas had not been in his father's room since he passed away.

Thomas got up and walked back to his father's bedroom. As he walked through the doorway, he took in all the memories of his father. Along the wall were dusty photos hanging of his father and mother when they were much younger. They were filled with happiness, and it was peculiar to think of what his father and mother were like before he had a clear memory of them. Thomas picked up his parents' wedding picture off the dresser and looked at his mother's eyes. They were so full of life

Thomas's father's closet seemed untouched since the days before his mother's accident. His shirts were neatly pressed and smelled of the musk aftershave he would wear on Sunday mornings. His shoes were neatly placed side by side on the closet floor, and his fedoras hung on a hat rack in the corner of the room. Thomas pulled out one of his father's button down collared shirts and put it on. He walked over to the mirror and examined his appearance. What he saw surprised him. The person in the mirror was no longer a boy but a man. As he looked into his own eyes, the harshness of his inner feelings flashed through the light reflecting off the mirror. All he could see was his father. He didn't want to be his father. He didn't want to give up and blame someone else for his own fate. He wanted to be something more. Thomas took a deep breath and then unbuttoned the shirt and placed it back on the coat hanger. He sat down on the bed and placed his face into his hands. As his emotions overcame him, he prayed in his moment of weakness. When he finished his prayer, he lifted his eyes from his hands to look around at the pictures on the wall.

He looked from one photo to the next, and something from the corner of his eye caught his attention. Thomas looked down, and under the back corner of the dresser, he noticed something peeking from behind it. He got up off the bed and bent down and pulled out an old dusty notebook that had fallen behind the dresser. Thomas opened it to the first page. It was dated October 16, 1946.

> Today is a very special day in the Krauss' home. Today we found out that there will be a new addition in the Krauss family next July! We are so excited to bring such a precious gift into this world. We are so blessed as a family, and I thank my God I get to experience being a mother. It has always been a dream of mine to experience the love of being a mother. God is so good to our family!

Thomas stopped reading there. He could feel the happiness in the words on the paper. He flipped through the pages and could tell that this was his mother's notebook. Tears came to his eyes. However, his thoughts were interrupted by a knock on the door. He sat the notebook down and walked to the front door. He opened it, frustrated, and immediately wiped his eyes, thinking his cloudy vision was deceiving him.

"Hello, Thomas."

There was Emily at his front door. He was surprised to see her up here. "Hey, what are you doing up here?"

Emily smiled shyly. "Well, my father had just mentioned you may come to dinner this evening. I just stopped by to see if you were coming or not because I need to know how much food I should cook," Emily said quietly.

"Oh." Thomas's awkwardness came off a little rudely, although it was unintentional.

"I'm sorry if I bothered you. I probably shouldn't have come up here." Emily started to leave the porch. Her cheeks blushed from embarrassment.

"No! It's okay." Thomas stepped out on the porch and grabbed Emily's hand to stop her from leaving. He quickly let go, and he too was embarrassed. "I mean…it's okay you came up here to ask. I understand," Thomas said as sternly and dryly as possible.

Emily smirked. She could see that his cheeks were flushing. "Okay, so will you be coming?" She raised her eyebrows.

"Yes'm, I will, just if it's okay with you." Thomas's eyes came to meet Emily's.

She smiled. "Well, I wouldn't have come up here if I didn't want you comin', now would I?" Emily turned and headed off the porch and back down the mountain toward town. Just before she reached out of Thomas's sight, she turned and smiled at him. Thomas didn't smile until she went over the hillside. Although it was a brief encounter, Thomas, for the first time, questioned his feelings about this girl. She made him feel like nothing in his life was wrong.

Thomas enjoyed his time with the Krauss family. It was the first time Thomas had been able to eat a good meal for a while. He particularly enjoyed the company of Emily, especially when she looked up from the table at him with those big green eyes. Emily let her hair out of its bun for dinner. Her curly black hair fell to the curve of her hips. Thomas would have to be careful not to choke on his food at times. Even though Thomas was rough around the edges, he was a kindhearted individual. It took time for Thomas to actually speak to Emily in the form of a conversation. After a couple months, he could actually put his feelings into words and tell Emily about some of his past. Emily would listen intently to Thomas. Sometimes she would laugh, and sometimes she would cry. Either way, Thomas appreciated her attention. Nobody had ever listened to him before.

CHAPTER 3

Rough Draft

One day, Thomas decided to take Emily somewhere he had never taken anyone. All his life, Thomas had wandered around the woods in the hills around town. When he was a young boy, he ran across an abandoned car someone had driven to the top of a mountain that overlooked the entire town of East Lynn. It was an old navy-blue Plymouth Coupe. The front and back windshields were still intact, and the windows even rolled down. Thomas had made it his very own spot to sit and think when his father came home drunk or his mother was having a bad day. Thomas loved to sit in the old car and pretend he was flying away from the sleepy town below. He imagined the wind blowing past his face. Sometimes he would go so fast the wind nearly took his breath away.

He had brought a few books he had found outside the barbershop and stored them under the driver's seat. One book was full of pictures of the big cities in America. Thomas imagined himself flying through Chicago down Washington Street or New York City, with all the lights shining brightly on the massive buildings. On rainy days, he would sit and look at the sleepy town and watch the water run through the creek and trickle over the rocks. The car was parked by an old pine tree, and the ground was always covered with the needles from years past. The scene was serene. The leather still smelled like it was fresh out of the factory. It was a museum to Thomas's imagination. Thomas guessed someone had abandoned it long ago.

This spot was one Thomas had shared or showed to no one else. His only companion through the years had been his imagination. For Thomas to bring Emily to this spot was an outward gesture of compassion because this spot meant so much to him. It was full of past memories, the only escape Thomas had ever had from the chains of his life.

Thomas held Emily's hand as they went up an old hunting trail and then followed the natural runoff of the mountainside where rainwater had cascaded down the hill for thousands of years. The simplistic beauty of the tall beech trees and oaks that stretched out of the ancient earth shaded the land with an eerie and almost magical curiosity. This curiosity blew as the wind did, shuddering the leaves and making the woods seem like one amazingly powerful breath, breathed out of the lungs of God himself. Thomas had grown to respect these hills that overlooked the town. They offered him a peace that no person ever could. With Emily by his side, he felt complete in a sense. She and the woods were one and the same. Both were majestic in their presence, powerful and beautiful, but both had a gentleness that comforted him. Thomas had never felt so whole in all his life.

After following the runoff, they reached the pine thicket. The pines offered a shield in the forest and seemed to hide the abandoned car well. A person couldn't see the car from town because it sat back in the darkness of the pines.

"What is this place, Thomas?"

"This is my abode," Thomas replied as he looked past the car to the smoky town below.

"I had no idea this place even existed," Emily replied as she began to smile.

"It doesn't," Thomas replied, and he smiled at Emily.

"Oh, I wouldn't tell a soul, Thomas," Emily said as her eyes widened.

Thomas smiled a big smile. "I know you wouldn't." He turned back to face the town. "This place is the only freedom I've had all my life." He brought his eyes down to the ground beneath him. "This is the only place I call my own. Nobody comes up here to beat me or harass me. That old car has been friendlier to me than my own flesh and blood."

Emily walked toward Thomas and laid her head on Thomas's shoulder.

"I've never brought anybody up here before. Nobody has meant enough to me to show 'em this place."

Emily brought her big green eyes up to look Thomas in the eyes. As Emily looked up at him, she noticed he had a rugged look about him. If she looked deep enough, though, she could see he was begging to love her. Thomas's eyes showed what raw emotion he felt for her. His heart was as swelled as a ripe watermelon, and it gushed for her. His love poured out from his soul from his eyes, and instantly Emily felt something she never had before.

Could this be what love feels like? Emily thought to herself. She touched Thomas on the face and drew her hand down to his chest. Thomas's heart was beating rapidly. He clenched his jaw and attempted to swallow.

"Emily, I love you," he said dryly.

It was hard for Thomas to feel all this emotion. He had been hardened, and his emotions were trained to be like stone. His eyes, however, showed his every feeling, and Emily smiled slightly as she grabbed Thomas's hand. She pulled him toward the darkness of the pines, and they both disappeared into the thicket.

The next couple months seemed like a dream to Thomas. He and Emily grew closer, and the fog that seemed to consume Thomas's mind was lifted. Thomas often thought about his father and how, even though he was a drunkard, he loved and missed both his mother and father. Emily made Thomas forget about all the bad in his life and saw nothing but the good.

The winter soon turned into spring, and the snow melted and gave way to new birth in the surrounding hills. The birds sang their new song, and the creek turned muddy from the melting frost and snow patches that dissipated from the hills that engulfed the smoky town beneath it.

Thomas sat on the Krauss' front porch swing and looked out over the field where new grass began to grow in place of where the previous year's corn grew. The morning dew was glistening from the orange sun peeking through the pink clouds. Two deer hastily edged their way out of the new growth to the openness of the morning fog and grazed steadily from one end of the field to the next. Thomas lit up a cigarette as the deer disappeared back into the forest. There was a lot on his mind from the past few weeks. There were a lot of emotions and changes going on inside him. Thomas thought about how similar the snow and ice that had melted from inside him was to that of the snow and ice in these mountains. It flooded the streams and rivers over as his heart had inside him. Thomas didn't know how to take all this emotion, but he liked it. It felt dangerous to him to leave all his hope in the palms of another person, but he loved Emily with everything inside him. It made Thomas weary to think what would happen if Emily left him or changed her mind about what she had felt over the past few weeks. He wanted to ask Emily how she felt, but chose not to because he was afraid he would insult her.

Thomas took one last puff from his cigarette and flicked it off the front porch. The front screen door creaked open, and he looked up to see Emily standing there with her hair down wearing a flower-printed nightgown. She had a smile on her face, and her big green eyes gleamed as they danced to Thomas's.

"Good morning." Thomas stood up and walked across the porch to Emily. He ran his hands through Emily's sleek black hair, then kissed her forehead.

"Thomas, I have to talk with you about something. It's about me going away to college." Emily was cut short by her mother's heels clicking down the stairs.

"Good morning, you two. Emily, will you come and help me get breakfast ready?"

Emily looked at Thomas. He had a bewildered look about him.

Thomas was confused. He stood at the doorway and looked back out across the field. The magic that the sunrise brought was gone. In the back of his mind, he knew all this was too good to be true, but his swollen heart drowned out whatever doubts or troubles he knew lay in the not-so-distant future.

Thomas skipped breakfast and headed up the old mountain to his thinking spot inside the dusty old Hudson. As Thomas got to the top of the hill, he looked over the sleepy old town and watched as cars drove on the streets below. The whistle of a distant train could be heard over the wind sweeping through the greenery of the pine trees above him. The wind seemed to brush against Thomas, bringing his mind back to the many times he stood atop this mountain and looked over the town. Nothing ever changed except for the trees that swayed with the cool spring breeze. Thomas went to the passenger's side and opened the door of the car. He reached under the seat and pulled out an old stainless steel flask. "Just me and you, old buddy. We've had a hell of a time together, ain't we?"

Thomas unscrewed the lid and plopped down on the hood and took a swig from the flask. The old whiskey burned all the way down into Thomas's belly and warmed him up a bit. He thought about what life would be like once Emily left for college. She would come in for the holidays, but most of the time, Thomas would be alone to face his problems in silence. This scared him. The thought of losing the one thing he loved seemed to make his spirit sink back into that shadow of a hole in his chest. He had no job and no place to call home. He had to find a way to get back on his feet, but the mines were the only job around besides the clerks at the local stores.

As Thomas sat there on the sun-warmed metal, he slowly began to realize that this dream he had been living was about to end as quickly as it had begun. Once Emily went off to college, Thomas would go back to stay by himself, and things would slowly sink back into the misery he drowned in before. He closed his eyes and dreamed of what life might be like with Emily. It seemed as if no darkness could blacken out her light. She was a living answered prayer, and Thomas was about to see the only thing he had ever loved leave to have a better life. He knew he was not good enough for Emily. Emily had money, nice clothes, and people enjoyed her company. Thomas was poor; he was an outcast and had no future. His daydreams seemed to remind him of the harsh reality of the situation. Visions of the past beatings and harsh words filled his mind. His pain came back to him. The cold and emptiness began to return to the recently warmed vessel he called his heart. The terror of living the rest of his life as Thomas Bailey gripped him yet again. Thomas took another swig of alcohol and then descended down the hillside back to the sleepy town resting below.

"Hey, son."

Thomas could hear God speaking to him.

"Son, are you all right?"

Thomas yelled out again.

"Son, wake up!"

Thomas was abruptly awakened and felt sheer panic sweep over his body.

"Son, good grief. I thought you were about to hop right out of bed and jump out the winda."

"What are you doing here?" There beside him sat the town mortician, James Avery. "Did I die or something?" Thomas asked.

"Well, no, son, you are not dead to my knowledge," said Mr. Avery as he switched the chaw from one cheek to the other.

"Oh…well, I figured that'd be the only reason you'd be in my house sitting by my bed," Thomas said.

"Well, your door was wide open, so I figured I'd let myself in. Actually, I came to ask you a question, son." Mr. Avery pulled out a twist of tobacco and bit off what seemed to Thomas the entire thing. "You see, the government is coming in and buying a lot of land around here. Word is, they're going to build a dam and flood the town out. Somethin' about flood control. I dunno what they're talkin' bout. There are a lot of graves that need a-movin', though, and I've been given the rights to dig 'em up. I was a-wonderin if you'd be interested in helpin' me out." Mr. Avery chewed on his tobacco slowly. "I'll pay ya for it."

Thomas sat and thought about it for a minute. He had no job and didn't know what the future held for him. "Well, sir, I was thinking about going and trying to get my job at the mines back," Thomas said.

"Well, that'd be all right if it wasn't shutting down, son."

Thomas was taken aback. "Shutting down? The mines are shutting down?"

"Yasser, they've 'bout run outta coal, and the railroad ain't a-goin' to be a-comin' into town much anymore either. So, son, would ya be interested in my offer?"

Thomas sat up uncomfortably in his bed. He didn't have many options, so why not? Thomas stuck his hand out. "When do I start?"

* * * * *

Thomas woke up the next morning bright and early. He headed over to the convenience store and grabbed a pack of smokes. His dreams had been consumed with things he could do with the money he would make moving all the graves. There were plenty of them. He might go buy a car so he could visit Emily or maybe even tickets to go see a show in Huntington. The possibilities were endless. The only thing that was worrying him was the distance Emily seemed to be placing between them lately. He just couldn't figure out what he had said or done that caused her to want the separation.

As he entered the convenience store, he noticed the local bullies in the back all huddled around the television.

"Hello, Thomas, what can I get for you today? Just the usual pack of smokes?" Jay the storekeeper asked.

"Yes, sir." Thomas looked back to keep an eye on Zack and his lowlife cult of followers. They seemed transfixed on the television. "Say, what are they watching back there?" Thomas asked the storekeeper.

"Well, last night they announced on the news that they would be implementing the draft on young men from the ages of eighteen to thirty years old. I'm guessing they're explaining now how that's going to work because it'll affect all you boys here, unless you plan on attending college." The storekeeper's eyes looked up at Thomas as he finished his sentence.

"Ha!" Thomas chuckled as he placed a cigarette in between his lips. "Well, sir, even if I did go over there, ain't no gook going to kill me," Thomas said as he walked out of the store. "You have yourself a great day, Jay." Thomas headed across town toward the graveyard where about ten men had already started digging.

"You're late, boy!" Mr. Avery spat as tobacco juice dribbled down his lip to his chin. "Grab a shovel and starta diggin'."

After work, Thomas headed straight over to the Krauss home in the valley just south of town. As he approached, he passed Mr. Krauss in his old 1950 Chevy 3100. Thomas nodded and squinted as the dust blew up in his face. As he reached the house, Emily was not there to greet him like usual. Mrs. Krauss was there in her place. "Hello, Thomas. How are you on this beautiful day?"

"Good, ma'am. I just got finished with work for the day."

"Oh, really? Where are you working?"

"Mr. Avery came and asked me to help move graves from the cemetery. He said something about the government buying up all the land to build a dam."

"Oh, is that right? Well, come on in. Emily isn't here right now, but I would like to have a word with you."

Thomas nodded and headed up the wood stairs into the Krauss farmhouse. Thomas walked over and took a seat on a wood chair in the corner of the room. Mrs. Krauss followed him and took a seat on the sofa beside him. She looked at Thomas's face and put her hands neatly on her lap as she pursed her lips.

"Thomas, I know that you and Emily have grown fond of each other over the past few months." Mrs. Krauss turned to look out the window toward the fields. "Thomas, have you ever noticed how animals of the forest seem to stay with their own kind?"

Thomas looked puzzled. "Yes, ma'am," he said softly.

"You know why that is?" Mrs. Krauss asked.

"Well, I'd guess because it's natural for them, ma'am."

"You are absolutely right, Thomas, because it's natural. Some things, however, don't make sense, and they end up being impure or lost." Mrs. Krauss got up off the couch and headed toward the door. Her words slowly sank into Thomas. He could feel his blood pressure rising. "Think about how bad it would be if something you love were to be lost, Thomas. Wouldn't you want what was best for what you loved so dearly?"

Thomas felt sick inside. Mrs. Krauss's words burned in his heart and in his mind. Thomas no longer felt welcome at the Krauss house.

He stood up and faced Mrs. Krauss. He was infuriated but held his tongue. He nodded and walked quickly out the door. As he exited the home, Mr. Krauss had just pulled back into the driveway.

"Hey, Thomas, how are you doing, buddy?"

Thomas looked ahead, avoiding eye contact with Mr. Krauss. He said nothing and then ran back down the dirt road toward town. As Mr. Krauss walked up to the porch, Mrs. Krauss watched with squinting eyes. "I wonder what's got into him?"

Mrs. Krauss lay silent for a while, then started back into the house. "He must have realized he belonged somewhere else."

Mr. Krauss looked at Mrs. Krauss, confused, and then looked back down the dusty road. Thomas had already run out of sight.

Thomas barely saw Emily that summer. She had spent most of it helping her father at the church house. She would always smile when she saw Thomas, and he would have to turn his eyes away from her. On the inside, his heart was crumbling into pieces, though his pride wouldn't let him show his grief. His dreams of himself and Emily being together had nearly diminished, and Thomas put all his frustrations into his work. He had nobody to answer to but himself.

As the months passed, the digging crew seemed to dwindle down by the week, and soon it was just Thomas and Mr. Avery left moving headstones. Mr. Avery always talked and told stories about the old days when he owned a farm and his wife was still alive. She had passed away when she was younger from pneumonia. Mr. Avery still spoke of her adoringly as if she was waiting for him back home. Thomas just listened, never saying too much while trying to relate his own problems to Mr. Avery's past battles. One thing that Mr. Avery always spoke about was the life of Jesus. Thomas listened to the stories, and he marveled at how great the authors of the Bible were. Thomas started to actually enjoy listening to Mr. Avery. Thomas became so interested he took up reading the Bible.

Thomas sat most nights alone trying to figure his life out. He didn't know what was next, but with the town dying, the mines shut down, and everyone selling their land, he figured soon he might look at moving out of this town himself. Soon Thomas and Mr. Avery's work was complete, and they had successfully moved all the graves just as the last week of summer came to a close. It had been nearly two months since he had last spoken to Emily. Although the distance between them seemed to grow, she was always there waiting for him in his dreams when he fell asleep at night.

Thomas woke up early Saturday morning and headed to the convenience store to get him a pack of cigarettes. A fog had set in on the town, and it made the town seem desolate as he walked on the streets. The nearby creek trickled by, and the whine of the local sawmill blade was the only obstructive sound inside this seemingly timeless valley. As Thomas got to the store, he was nearly knocked over when he reached the top of the wood stairs by Zack Lindsey. He rushed off the porch, stumbling and sobbing down the gravel road, whimpering like a beat dog.

"What in the…" As Thomas watched Zack run off, Mr. Vaughn, the store owner, exited the front door. "What's going on with him?"

"Not too sure, son. I just handed him a letter, and when he opened it, he got all torn up and ran like a bat out of hell outta here."

"Who was it from?"

"Well, he left the envelope lying in there. Let's find out."

Thomas and Mr. Vaughn went into the store and picked up the envelope lying off the floor: "Department of Defense." Thomas looked at the envelope and thought of what it could be.

"Hey, speaking of which, I have a letter for you also."

"I got mail?" Thomas never got mail.

Mr. Vaughn walked over to a stack of letters. Thomas noticed as he searched through the stack that all the letters appeared to be the same on the outside with the Department of Defense seal on each one.

"Ahh, here we go." Mr. Vaughn handed Thomas his letter.

Thomas looked at the letter, and a sense of curiosity mixed with dread filled his gut.

"Are you gonna open it?"

Thomas preferred to open it privately because whatever was in it just made the toughest guy in town cry like a child. It was hard to say what it would do to Thomas. Thomas decided to just tear it open because his pride wouldn't let him be weak in front of anyone. He opened the seal and pulled out the cream-colored letter and unfolded it. Thomas read the first few sentences and felt his stomach flip upside down. Now he understood why Zack had torn out of the store in such a horrible manner. Thomas nearly lost his balance and caught himself on the store's countertop before he reached the ground.

"What is it, boy?" Mr. Vaughn grabbed Thomas's arm and helped him up. "Son, what's the matter? What is in that letter?"

Thomas looked at Mr. Vaughn. His lips were blue, his face pale. "I'm going to Vietnam."

CHAPTER 4

A Burning Past

Thomas held the letter tightly in his palm. It wasn't him that clenched the letter so tightly as much as it was his fear. After all he had dealt with in his life, and after some good things started to come, it was slowly all turning back into bad. As fearful and heartbroken as he was, though, he dared not show any sort of emotion as Zack had. He turned toward Mr. Vaughn. Mr. Vaughn had a stern look on his face. It was borderline sorrow, but he quickly realized his feelings were outwardly showing and changed his expression to a smile.

"It'll be all right, boy. Hell, everybody is going over there anyways. Wouldn't wanna miss the party, would you?" Mr. Avery said sarcastically.

Thomas's voice cracked into a fake chuckle. "Yeah, you know me. I love parties." Thomas looked at Mr. Vaughn as a million things came flooding in his mind. "Well, sir, I guess I best be headin' out of here." Thomas walked away as Mr. Vaughn watched him leave the store with sorrowful eyes.

Thomas stepped out on the porch of the store and looked around at the dusty town around him. There were the local older fellas out whittling sticks in front of the courthouse. The meter lady passed by parked cars, checking how much time was left. Thomas took a deep breath. He felt alone. It was as if he went unseen in this world. He put his head down and walked to the outskirts of town. There was only one place he wanted to be, and that was with Emily, but now his love had become even more complicated as the odds of him coming home from war alive were very slim.

Thomas finally reached the top of the mountain and sat in his favorite thinking spot. He shook his head in disbelief as he peered out at the surrounding mountains. What was he supposed to say to Emily now? Thomas got halfway up the mountain and looked around at the wilderness that surrounded him. The mountains had certain purity to them that struck Thomas nearly every time he entered into its tranquility. They went unblemished due to man's negligence. It was hard to fathom that he would be going to fight in a war against people he didn't even know. He imagined this would be one of the last times he would walk through these woods and experience this type of peace. Violence was not in his nature, although it did seem to follow him throughout his life.

As Thomas sat and let the reality of his circumstances sink in, he glanced around at his surroundings. It had not occurred to him that there was a trail hidden beneath the underbrush off the dirt road to his home. He sat and wondered how, after all these years, he had not noticed it. His curiosity led him into the brush and into the surrounding beech trees. The hills were filled with old trails from the thousands of years the Indians roamed freely. They were formed long before the white man had come and ravaged God's original design.

As Thomas walked, the feeling of déjà vu passed through him. This place felt familiar. After a few hundred yards, the trees became thin, and the underbrush cleared into a grassy knoll. There in the clearing sat an old walnut tree. Its branches were jagged and leafless. Down the middle was a large crack from top to bottom, and the roots twisted and crawled from beneath the soil. There by the tree sat a large stone. It was a peculiar feeling to see such an eerie scene in these serene woods.

Thomas walked over to the rock and placed his hands on the old tree. Although it looked lifeless, it was as sturdy as any tree in the forest, almost as if nature had preserved the wood from destruction. Thomas walked around the tree and up the embankment that surrounded the large rock beside the tree. He stopped hesitantly as he noticed empty glass liquor bottles all around lying on the ground. The bottles all had the same label. It just so happened to be the same whiskey his father had drunk for many years. As Thomas looked at the whisky bottles thrown about, he noticed a worn-out trail heading up the mountain toward the direction of his house. As he passed by the rock, he noticed some initials engraved into the heavy-looking stone. It was a heart with the initials *JTK* above *SJK*.

John Thomas Krauss and Sarah Jade Krauss, Thomas thought to himself. The eeriness of the place now was understood. His mother and father must have come here together at some point. How had he overlooked that trail after all these years tromping through the woods? Thomas turned and looked back at the old tree that stood preserved in this hidden knoll, and a strange thought came into his head. *What if that tree had been struck by lightning?* Thomas gazed at the roots twisting and the crack down the center of it. *What if this is the place my mother died?*

Thomas pushed the idea from his head and headed back up the trail. It led him right to a ditch line that trailed up to his cabin. He couldn't understand how he had missed it after all these years. His curiosity had led him to discover an intriguing place from an unknown history of his mother and father. The ideas and dreams of the day they carved their initials into the stone brought sad thoughts to Thomas's mind. Although he didn't remember much about when his father and mother were younger, it allowed Thomas to imagine. Maybe this place was special to them. That's what Thomas wanted to think. Even though it was a long shot, Thomas thought he had found the spot where his mother had passed. After thinking and feeling down, he decided to pull out his mother's journal again. He flipped to where he had left off many months ago.

Thomas has grown so much in the past two years.
He is so beautiful to me. I see his father in him.

The words started to gnaw at Thomas for a minute, but he continued to read.

He is such a happy boy. He loves to play out in the woods, and he won't leave his father's side.

Everyone at church thinks he looks like me, though. I can see in his eyes that he will be a good man someday. I just want him to grow in the Lord and to be a light for the entire world to see just how good our God really is. He is such a blessing. God has truly blessed this family.

Thomas had to drop the journal on the bed.

I just want him to grow in the Lord and to be a light for the entire world to see just how good our God really is. He is such a blessing. Thomas's stomach dropped. He was the last thing on this earth that could be considered a light for God. He felt like a failure. The words played over in his mind as shame and guilt of all his past replayed in his head. He thought about the words he had said to Mr. Krauss and his father. If he died right now, what would people remember him as? More important was the question, what would people remember about his family? He answered his own question: *nothing good.* That's what people saw him as. Even though he hadn't realized it, there were many situations in which he could have been a better person. He thought back about how good of a person his mother was. He was tarnishing her godly memory by falling into the same life his father had lived. There was no way he was going to leave this town and possibly die in some far-off land and leave his mother's memory tarnished because of his own bitterness.

Thomas sat rocking in his mother's old rocking chair, staring around at the old cabin. It, along with the land his grandfather had passed down, was about all he had to call his own. The problem was all the bad memories he had to go along with it. He would be leaving soon, and when he came back, this cabin would be what he returned to. Thomas shook his head. What if he didn't come home? Thomas stood up. He didn't want himself or his father to be what people remembered. Instead, he wanted them to remember his mother, who gave their name pride in the Lord and love because that was what she gave to everyone else.

Thomas went back into the bedroom and grabbed his mother's journal. He walked back out, and that was when he made the decision. Thomas walked out of the cabin and walked to the shed where his father kept his rusty old tools that hadn't been used in years. There on the dirt floor sat some old gasoline cans. He grabbed all the cans and walked back to the cabin and walked up the stairs back through the old rusty hinged door. He took one more look around, then began to pour the gasoline all over the house as quickly as possible. He left everything. Everything except the journal he had found. Once all the gasoline was poured, he walked outside and took one last look at the old cabin, then struck a match, igniting his entire past into a ball of flames. The heat was intense. Thomas watched the flames as they danced out of the window frames. He could feel that same burn inside him as his past disappeared along with the framework of the cabin. Thomas watched the entire cabin burn to mere ashes on the ground. After it was gone, he walked to the little shed and pulled out an axe, then headed down the ditch to the grassy knoll.

Once Thomas reached the grassy knoll, he got a good grip on the axe and took a swing into the big tree. It was as solid a tree as any Thomas had ever chopped into. Swing after swing, the cuts made little impact on the large tree. The determination, though, that Thomas had wouldn't let his frail arms stop swinging the axe. Every blow was an outward thrust of his built-up emotions. As he chopped, he thought about his mother and how he would honor her. Thomas came to the tree from sunup to sundown for nearly a week, but he finally managed to chop the tree down. When the final blow came, Thomas swung with every bit of strength he had left. His hands were bleeding from all the blisters, but he worked through the pain and wrapped his hands in an old ripped T-shirt. His clothes were soaked with sweat, and his body ached. As the tree fell down, so did Thomas on the cool earth beneath his feet. As he looked at the tree, he saw what past was left of his mother and of his family.

Thomas worked tirelessly for the next month on the grassy knoll. He cut the wood and carved all day long, week after week. He stayed out of town and slept each night right beside the old tree in the grass. Soon his mother's memory started to take shape. It was difficult for Thomas to mold the shapes he wanted, but sometimes it would rain and soften the tough wood and give his aching muscles a rest. After nearly four weeks, he cut the last strip of wood off his work and carried each one up the mountainside. While working for those few weeks, Thomas had thought a lot about Mrs. Krauss's words. They cut him deeply, but the love he felt for Emily still burned inside him more than it ever had. He hadn't seen her in a while. He figured now her feelings were probably not the fondest for him.

There were many things Thomas wanted to right that he had done wrong before he left home, but the one thing he must do was talk with Emily and tell her his feelings. He respected Mrs. Krauss, but there was no way he was going away without telling Emily he loved her. As the week ended, Thomas decided to go down and clean himself up. In the morning, he had to let Emily know how he felt. Time was running out for him, so he headed into town to the local inn and got a room for the night. He hoped the morning would leave him a fresh start. As Thomas lay down and closed his eyes, he started to think. His thoughts soon faded into darkness as he fell asleep.

CHAPTER 5

When It Rains, It Pours

Thomas didn't feel welcome at the Krauss home anymore, so he figured he would try and stay at the local inn until he could figure something else out. Mrs. Krauss had made her feelings clear, and Thomas was bitter, but believed she was right. Thomas was not worthy of a woman like Emily. Thomas got his room and sat on the bed with all of Emily's words flowing through his mind. He loved Emily, but she would soon be on to better things than this small sleepy town. As Thomas started to dose off, there was a soft knock on the door.

"Thomas, can I come in?"

Thomas knew that voice from anywhere. He walked to the door and unlatched the lock. There was Emily. He opened the door to let her inside. She came in and looked the room over as Thomas shut the door behind her.

"Why didn't you tell me you weren't seeing me anymore, Thomas?" Emily turned to Thomas with a stern look on her face.

Thomas walked over and sat down on the bed. He stared at the floor and tried to think of what he would say to Emily.

"You know you're always welcome in our home."

He looked up at Emily. She could tell he wanted to say something to the contrary, but he held his tongue. "Well, are you going to give me an answer or leave me wondering?" Emily's face bore a look of anger and confusion.

"How did you know I was staying here anyways?" Thomas attempted to change the subject, but Emily was persistent.

"It's a small town, Thomas. Now answer me, or I'm leaving."

Thomas looked at her, and he could see Emily's eyes starting to fill with tears. Thomas didn't want to talk about what her mother had said to him. He wanted what was best for her, and deep down, he felt the same way about him as Emily's mother did.

"I just figured I was ruining my welcome staying and not contributing much to your father and mother. Just wanted to get out on my own again, I guess."

Emily stared at Thomas. "Thomas, what is this really all about?"

"It's about me not wanting to be a burden on you and your future. It's about me not wanting to be a burden on your family." Thomas walked over to the window and looked down on the street below. "I know that you have a lot going for you, and I don't want to drag you down."

Emily walked over to Thomas. "Thomas, I love you. You're not a burden to anyone."

"Look at me, Emily. I'm just a poor hillbilly. You, look at you. You're beautiful, you're smart, you have a wonderful family. I'm not going to get in the way of that because I don't have any of those things. I will just bring you down."

Emily's eyes filled with tears. It was all Thomas could stand. Inside, he wanted to be with Emily more than anything, and he loved her deeply, but he felt he wasn't good enough; and deep down, he knew Emily's mother was right.

"I'm sorry, Emily, but I can't see you anymore."

Emily looked at Thomas, and tears began to stream down her cheeks. "I don't understand, Thomas." Emily grabbed Thomas's arm. It was the most difficult thing Thomas ever had to do.

"Just leave, Emily."

Emily looked at Thomas, and her sadness was replaced with anger. She stormed out of the room and slammed the door behind her.

Thomas's dreams were filled with Emily that night. He just couldn't seem to get her out of his head. Her mother's words echoed throughout the visions of Emily's face, softly playing on the inside of Thomas's eyelids. Although they were pleasant visions, the words cut like a knife. Thomas's pleasant visions soon grew dark with clouds, and he found himself alone in a field with rain falling upon his cheeks. Thunder rolled on the hills ahead of him, and strong winds blew against his body. Thomas could hear the hum of something zipping by his ears. The ground shook beneath him, and his knees trembled. There were loud booms in the distance. His dreams were cut short as he became aware this place was not a good place for him to be. Thomas awoke abruptly in a cold sweat. The loud knocking at his door startled him.

"Thomas!" A loud clap of thunder made his iron-framed bed vibrate. "Thomas, wake up!" Thomas recognized the voice as Emily's. He quickly got out of bed and walked quickly to the door. He opened it to see Emily standing there soaking wet and water dripping off her small chin.

"Why are you soaking wet? Come inside, I'll get you a towel."

"Thomas…," Emily's voice was quivering. "Ma is in trouble."

Thomas turned and looked at Emily. She was very shaken up. He was confused and scared at the same time.

* * * * *

Thomas and Emily swept down the stairs at the inn. Once they reached the first floor, Thomas could see water running nearly half-way up the walls. "What the…" Thomas's confusion now turned to concern for Emily's safety, but Emily seemed determined and unafraid of what was happening. "Emily, what is going on?"

Emily jumped into the water and began to swim for the front door at the end of the long hallway.

"Emily!" Thomas jumped in the water after her. The water was cold and muddy. The lights in the inn flickered on and off as Thomas struggled to keep up with Emily.

As Thomas and Emily finally reached the entrance, Emily shoved with all her might against the door and finally pushed it open. Thomas looked out into the street to see Main Street, which once was a gravel road, turned into a rushing river. Thomas couldn't believe his eyes. The rain that fell seemed to drown out the surrounding mountains, and people were swimming for their lives to reach higher ground. Thunder shook the building and lightning struck on the hillside that Thomas once called home.

"Where is your mother?" Thomas asked, turning to Emily. Emily was trembling. Thomas couldn't decipher the look on her face or the water that flowed down her cheeks from the tears that filled her eyes. "Emily, where is your mother? Look at me." Thomas grabbed Emily and looked her in the eyes. "Emily, where is your mother?"

"She's trapped inside our house."

Thomas pushed through the water as quickly as he could toward a passing johnboat. He held on to Emily with one hand and pushed the debris aside with the other. It seemed as if the hills had washed down into the valley, destroying the town as it passed. What once was a docile creek that flowed through town was now a river with no boundaries rushing through the once-dusty streets of East Lynn.

"Thomas? 'At you, boy?"

Thomas looked and saw the familiar face of Mr. Avery appear through the dense fog. "Mr. Avery, I need you to help me get to the Krauss farm."

"Well, boy, I don't think I can get down there in this little boat," Mr. Avery explained.

"Well, sir, you're gonna have to try."

Thomas quickly helped Emily get into the johnboat, and Mr. Avery swung the johnboat around toward the Krauss farm. The farm was situated in a small valley just south of town. The rolling hills from the town fell off into the valley, which just happened to be directly beside the flowing creek that was inside of a deep hollow carved out of the mountains. Thomas thought about the layout of the surrounding hills and the valley that lay below where the Krauss farm lay. He knew it would more than likely be the most treacherous water they would see.

"Mr. Avery, if you don't mind, I'd like to drop off Emily at the church." Thomas didn't look at Emily.

"Thomas, I'm going with you." Emily's eyes widened as she looked back to Mr. Avery. "Sir, I'm going with you all, so don't head toward the church."

"Emily, you're not coming." Thomas turned to Emily to see her eyes piercing into him. Her face bore a look of fierce determination.

"I will go, and you won't stop me!" Emily stated as her voice quivered.

"Emily, it's going to be extremely dangerous. I need you to stay here because"—Thomas thought quickly for a reason to try and change her mind—"because if you're in the boat, it will capsize once we pick up your mother. This little boat isn't meant for four grown adults. Right, Mr. Avery?" Thomas shot a look toward Mr. Avery.

Mr. Avery looked at Emily, then back to Thomas. "That's right, Thomas. It could endanger everybody if we put four people in this boat." Mr. Avery cleared his throat and tried his best to not make eye contact with Emily. Emily began to sob, and Thomas became concerned but concealed his worry. Although he loved Emily, he fought feelings of dislike and disregard for Mrs. Krauss. Her words replayed in Thomas's mind over and over. The thought of leaving her trapped crossed into his mind, but Thomas quickly scolded himself mentally for his feelings. He had to reach her for Emily.

Mr. Avery turned the boat south facing the outskirts of town. The current swiftly pushed the boat along through the town. As Thomas and Mr. Avery passed, there were people yelling for help on the rooftops as the water had submerged most of the buildings up to the second floor. "Don't worry, we will be back through here in a minute!"

Thomas didn't like leaving people behind, but his guess was that the Krauss farm was in much worse shape than the town. The elevation drop had to be fifty plus feet, and the water was already pushing the boat so fast the engine could barely keep up. Just as soon as Thomas and Mr. Avery reached the edge of town, the mountain that led down to the Krauss farm had disappeared. The only thing in sight was water and the adjacent mountain hundreds of yards away past the Krauss farm. The boat funneled down the hill as Mr. Avery pulled the prop out of the water.

"Don't wanna get hung up on the way down this, boy. We'll die if we capsize on this hill."

The current became so rapid that Thomas clung to the side of the boat as tightly as possible. Every chop in the water sent the two in midair, and water was intensely smashing into them from all angles. Thomas struggled to catch his breath as water pounded him again and again. What seemed like an hour since they started at the top of the hill had passed before the water leveled off, and when Thomas raised his eyes, he could barely believe what he saw. The valley that once held the Krauss' corn farm had vanished, and the only part that was visibly left was the very top of the roof of their once-beautiful Colonial-style farmhouse.

"Oh my God." Mr. Avery shakily raised to his feet. "Thomas, we're too late, son."

Thomas looked intently at the house for any sign of life. The odds were not in Mrs. Krauss's favor.

Mr. Avery turned the boat around the house as Thomas searched for any sign of life. The water pushed its way out the top of the windows of the house as tree branches raked across the side of the boat. Just as Thomas and Mr. Avery were making their last pass around, Thomas saw a hand surface out of the water and splash down back into the murky depths.

"There she is!"

Thomas jumped off the side of the boat and swam against the current. The water pushed him down the side of the house and under the surface. He tried his best to gasp for a breath every time his mouth reached the surface. He gagged and kept straining to get a breath. He finally was able to get a grip on a board along the side of the house and pull himself above the surface. He had been pulled to the other side of the house, away from where Mrs. Krauss had been. Thomas looked around as Mr. Avery struggled to get through all the debris on the surface of the water. "You all right, boy?"

"Yeah, did you see her again?" Thomas yelled.

"No, I didn't, son."

Thomas felt a tug on his leg and was dragged under the surface again. He felt with his hands, trying to reach anything to gain a grip.

His hand caught something soft, and it was in a moment of clarity that he realized it was a human hand. He grabbed for anything he could when he finally wrapped his arms around the body and kicked with all his strength to the surface. His head finally felt the cold air as his mouth gasped for oxygen. He pulled up on the torso he was holding as Mrs. Krauss's face, full of hair, surfaced. Her lips were blue and her face pale.

"Mr. Avery!" he yelled as he struggled to hold on to Mrs. Krauss as the current pushed against them, whipping them away from the house. As the house became smaller and smaller, Thomas's fear grew as he watched the trees around him pass by. The wind blew into his wet face, and sadness consumed him as he thought about Mrs. Krauss. As the house passed out of sight, Thomas looked at the waters flowing off the mountains. As his arms became weak and his fingers started to slip apart from around Mrs. Krauss, he heard a dull groan of that small engine on the back of Mr. Avery's boat. Thomas looked back as Mr. Avery whipped into sight from around the bend. His long beard was drenched, but his eyes were strong as the boat beat through the current and over the branches in its path. Thomas clung as tightly as he could to Mrs. Krauss as the boat inched closer to them. Just as Mr. Avery came within reach, Thomas felt a tug as his pants and then his head was pulled under the rushing water.

Thomas kicked with all his might to try and free his leg. The water was cold, and its power made Thomas helpless. Amid the powerful jerk of his leg, he had lost his grip on Mrs. Krauss. He felt for her, but there was only water that surrounded him. His thoughts returned to himself as he knew his time was running out. The breath he took in before he was pulled under was a short one, and his lungs felt as if they were going to explode from the pressure as the blood flow in his head rushed from the rest of his body. He felt down at his ankle to try and free himself of what was snagging him. There was a tree, and his foot was caught between two limbs. This was not a small tree as Thomas could not get his hands around the limb. He felt for his boot laces and pulled frantically at them as his ears started to ring from the pressure. He searched and searched. When he could finally hold his breath no more, he gave one last tug at the laces, and he was immediately pulled with the current. His head surfaced as he gasped for air, choking on the muddy water as he slapped around for something to grasp. Just as soon as he could open his eyes, he felt something strong grab his forearm as he was pulled from the water and dropped down on the hard surface of Mr. Avery's boat.

"Thought you was dead, boy."

Thomas looked up to see Mr. Avery standing over him. Rain dripped from his beard. and his blue eyes were looking over Thomas as if to check and make sure every piece of him was intact. Thomas quickly remembered as he tried to sit up that he had lost Mrs. Krauss. "Where is she?" Thomas looked around Mr. Avery toward the back of the boat. He scrambled to his knees and crawled past Mr. Avery to see the back of the boat. "Mr. Avery?" Thomas looked to Mr. Avery. Worry filled his eyes as guilt filled his heart.

"I let her go…I just couldn't hang on…"

"Thomas," Mr. Avery interrupted.

Thomas looked up to see Mr. Avery pointing back toward the house. Thomas turned his head to see Mrs. Krauss sitting on a tree limb on the hillside. Thomas started to cry as Mrs. Krauss waved from the distance.

"You did it, son." Mr. Avery bent down and slapped Thomas on the shoulder. "You did good, Thomas."

Thomas grabbed Mr. Avery and gave him a hug as the rain steadily fell on the both of them.

"Let's get back to town where it's safe now." Mr. Avery turned the boat around and headed for Mrs. Krauss. When they reached her, Thomas helped her aboard. She immediately hugged Thomas. There were no words exchanged between them. Thomas knew she finally respected him, but could see the regret and gratitude in her eyes. That was enough for him.

"All right, let's get out of here."

"Hold on, Mr. Avery." Thomas felt the need to be alone. His mind wandered as much as his emotions. The trauma from all that had just happened finally grasped him. "Can you let me off on the hillside, Mr. Avery?"

Mr. Avery scowled. "Son, why don't you come back with us and get checked out?"

Thomas looked up at Mr. Avery. "I need some time, Mr. Avery."

Mr. Avery looked at Thomas, and although he disagreed, he did as Thomas asked. He whipped the boat back around toward the hillside and pulled as close as he could to the bank. Thomas jumped off onto the muddy incline and wheeled around.

"Thank you."

Mr. Avery nodded in understanding and turned the steering wheel back around as Mrs. Krauss looked at Thomas. Thomas watched as the boat faded into the distance and out of sight. Thomas walked up the mountain and climbed into his old Plymouth. It was very quiet inside the old car. He looked out of the windshield at the flooded town. He tried to process all that had just happened, but his mind wouldn't let him.

CHAPTER 6

Farewell

The entire community seemed to make their way to the church for refuge as Thomas sat on the mountain overlooking the flooded town below. As he peered down, the once-smoky streets below had disappeared and were mere figments of the imagination as the rushing waters had consumed most of what was left in view. The church stood well out of the water as it peered out over the hillside on which it was built. As he took in the stress of what he had been through that day, it occurred to him that he had done far more than he thought himself capable of. While the other townspeople ran for higher ground, Thomas had been in the water over his head, trying to save a life. His love for Emily had given him a strength he didn't know he possessed. Unknowingly, he had traded his lack of confidence for sheer determination. As this realization came over him, a sense of pride filled him. He was doing what he had set out to do for his mother's name. But more than anything on his mind was setting things right with Emily. Now probably wouldn't be the best time to talk, though, after all her family had been through, and Mr. Krauss was very busy taking in the entire community.

Thomas sighed and watched the rain drip on his old car and trickle down the windshield. It was a needed peace. The responsibility that he eventually would have to grasp along with the day's tension had worn him down. As he lay with the seat back, taking it all in, the door slowly creaked open. Thomas sat up startled. There, soaking wet in the pouring rain, was Emily. Thomas looked into her eyes as the raindrops concealed her tears. He reached out with his hand, patiently waiting on her to take it. Her soft hand gently fell on Thomas's as she crawled inside the car with him and sat down on his lap. Thomas held Emily quietly for a while, not saying a word. There were no words needed. All that could be heard was the rain falling onto the windshield. All that could be felt was the agony of the separation they had endured.

As the night came and went and the sun began to rise, Thomas felt it was time to let Emily know what was about to take place in his life. As they watched the sun rise, Thomas looked into Emily's eyes. "I have something I need to tell you, Emily."

Emily's big green eyes were transfixed. She could feel Thomas's hesitation and was quiet with anticipation. "Yes?"

Thomas's heart began to race as his blood pressure rose. He was afraid to tell Emily in fear that she might leave him, but Thomas knew it was the right thing to do. Although he could have made Mrs. Krauss's words come back to haunt her, he chose not to. Instead, he gave her an explanation that wouldn't hurt Emily worse than he had to. "I received a letter a couple weeks ago."

Emily looked Thomas's face over as he struggled to spit out the next few words.

"There really is no other way to put it. I've been drafted." Thomas looked at Emily as tears began to swell in her eyes. She wept on Thomas's lap as Thomas did his best to console her.

"You can't go, Thomas. I need you."

Thomas looked at Emily, confused. "You need me? I thought you would just leave me once you heard."

"Leave you?" Emily looked up at Thomas as tears rolled off her cheeks. "Thomas, I have something I need to tell you also. I should have told you a while ago, but I didn't know how." She wiped the tears from her eyes and placed her hands on Thomas's cheeks. "You're going to be a father."

* * * * *

Slowly after a few days, the waters receded from the town and left behind nothing but a memory of what once was. The only trace of the flood's chaos was the mud-washed sidewalks and drift lines on the once-busy buildings in town. Many people walked back to their homes to find an empty vessel. Their homes were but a shell as they once were filled with life and love. As the people in the town came together to help one another, Thomas watched as masks of sadness covered all their faces. Thomas hadn't had a home in quite some time. His home had also been an empty vessel, and as he looked at the people who had ignored him most of his life, a strange sense of pity fell over him. They, for once, understood what he felt. Although he had always wished deep down for people to understand him, guilt and sorrow was in the place of the satisfaction he expected to feel. Seeing these people suffer as he had didn't make him feel satisfied as he anticipated. It pained him to see his town in shambles and the people so devastated. Thomas thought of ways he could help, but there wasn't much that could be done other than comfort the people who didn't have any family there to console them.

With the town in shambles and time running out, Thomas sat in his favorite thinking spot and looked out over the debris-filled creek that now merely trickled through the mountains and beside the small destroyed town he called home. He thought of any way he could help, but his mind was blank. He rubbed his temples as the tension of time and troubles seemed to overwhelm his thinking capabilities. As he sat and pondered, a brilliant idea came to his mind as his eyes came across the wood he had carved out of the old jagged tree he ran across. Thomas got up and walked over to the cedar slabs he had spent nearly two weeks carving out. He took the six slabs and nailed each piece on to another, forming three separate crosses. After he was finished, he carried each set over in front of his old thinking spot and started digging. He used ropes to pull the heavy slabs into position. His arms ached as he fought to balance the heavy wood. It took hours to put each piece into position. He finished right on time as the sun set behind the hills and night fell upon him.

Thomas had pondered many ways that he could help the people of his town, and in doing so, his mind seemed to always fall upon his mother. *What would my mother do to help?* In the old journal he found, his mother had mentioned that she wanted him to "let his light shine" onto the world. Thomas thought about these words a lot over the past couple of weeks, but as much as he thought, he couldn't understand what they meant. He knew that it wasn't a light in the literal sense, so what was his light? The answer came to him as he thought of what his mother seemed to always mention in her letters: her faith. As he thought of his mother and what her "light" seemed to consist of, it seemed to always bring back the fact that her faith was so strong in the Lord. As he connected the two, he realized his light wasn't something he had on his own. She was talking about the light of Jesus. This light she spoke of was showing the world how good God had been to her and can be to others if they have it. Thomas finally understood. It wasn't what he could do but rather how he could show other people the goodness of his mother's God. It was hard to think of showing a light inside him that reflected God because, truthfully, Thomas couldn't think of much God had done for him through most of his life. But the one thing he did have was Emily, and that seemed to wipe away all his bitterness.

As darkness covered the forest around him, Thomas knew what he had done on this mountain was surely letting his light shine. Thomas walked over to the old car and opened up the door and sat inside. There were only a couple days left before he had to leave Emily and this little town. Tomorrow would be the day he let his light shine.

Thomas cracked his eyelids open as the sun began to rise over the adjacent hillside. The birds chirped loudly in the surrounding pines. Thomas was happy he woke up early today. He had a lot to do in a short amount of time. He sat up in his seat to see his finished project there in front of him. As he looked it over, the power in such simplicity swelled his chest. Thomas got out of the car and took one last look at his project as he descended down the mountain.

Thomas reached town as the sun shone through the thick fog that had set in the night before. Emily had been staying at the church with her family. They lost almost everything in the flood, and the church was the only refuge most of the town had. He walked up the concrete steps and twisted the brass doorknob and pushed it open. There inside were a lot of people sleeping in the pews. Some of the older men who whittled in front of the courthouse sat around the coffeepot with Mr. Avery, talking as they always did. Most of the men had slept on the floor and let the women have the comfort of the pews. Thomas walked in and made his way around all the people still sleeping over to Mr. Avery.

"Where you been, boy? People's been worried 'bout ya.

"Well, I had some things I needed to take care of. Have you seen Mr. Krauss?"

Mr. Avery made his usual face when he was thinking. It reminded Thomas of the Popeye cartoons. His chin seemed to curl to his upper lip when his mind was functioning. "Yes, sir, he's getting breakfast ready, I do believe."

Thomas nodded to all the men standing around. "Thank you."

Thomas walked toward the back of the church. The back of the church was open with tall ceilings and tables set in rows. There were a few people setting chairs at the tables and others setting silverware out beside the plates. Over at the table with all the children was Emily. She was reading a story to all the kids. She looked up just in time to see Thomas as he made his way over to where Mr. and Mrs. Krauss sat.

"Hold on, children, I'll be right back." Emily laid the book down speedily and headed to try and see what Thomas was doing. "Thomas, is everything okay?" Emily walked beside Thomas. He was focused on making it to Mr. and Mrs. Krauss, who were waiting intently to see what exactly was going on.

Thomas stood in front of Mr. Krauss.

"Son." Mr. Krauss stuck out his hand to shake.

Thomas shook it quickly and took a deep breath. His heart was pounding, and he felt the heat of it in his head. He looked at Mrs. Krauss and then back to Emily. She looked confused and then grabbed his hand. "Thomas?"

Thomas turned and looked back at Mr. and Mrs. Krauss. "I came here to ask you for your daughter's hand in marriage." Thomas felt Emily's grip tighten. Mr. Krauss looked to the floor as Thomas assumed his mind must be wandering as the question sank into his brain.

Mrs. Krauss stepped forward and placed her hand on Mr. Krauss's shoulder. "Let's give it some time, Thomas." She looked at Thomas. "There has been a lot happening today. Let's just wait and—"

"Ma'am, I apologize to interrupt, but I don't have time to wait." Thomas wasn't leaving this church until he made his case. "In two weeks, I'll be going to join the military. I may never even come back," Thomas begged.

Emily placed her hand over her mouth as tears filled her eyes.

"I-I can't leave this place knowing I left the best thing I ever knew behind me—and never knowing what it was like to share something holy with that one good thing. Look, I have no money. I've got no job. Not much of anything, really. All I know is I love your daughter, and I'd do anything for her. I mean that. I will love her and take care of her any way I can. That's a promise."

Thomas's passion had gained the attention of the entire church.

"Ah, just let 'em get married."

Everyone in the church turned to the entranceway. There stood Mr. Avery. Water dripped off his big black beard. He addressed Mr. Krauss, "I mean, good grief, he saved your wife's life. You owe him one."

Mr. Krauss chuckled. "Ah, I guess you're right, Mr. Avery."

Mrs. Krauss blushed and walked out of the room. Emily smiled at Thomas. Thomas turned back and looked at Mr. Avery. He gave a small wink and then turned and walked back out into the storm.

Mr. Krauss looked Thomas over and then stuck his hand out. "Looks like we're going to be pretty busy within the next couple weeks."

Thomas smiled and shook his hand. "Thank you, sir."

Emily hugged Thomas and then her father.

"You'd better go speak with your mother. I think she's in a little bit of a shock right now," Mr. Krauss said.

Emily nodded and headed toward the back of the church.

"Thomas, we have some work to do around here. Why don't you help me get dry clothes and blankets for some of these people?" Mr. Avery handed Thomas a big stack of blankets.

"I'd be glad to."

In the following days, the water receded from the town. The once paved roads were now covered with mud as debris from the town's homes were now blanketing the banks of Twelvepole Creek. Most had lost everything they owned. Thomas helped the townspeople with cleaning up and salvaging all they could from each home. Thomas left the inn and returned to the old Plymouth. It was the only home untouched by the floodwaters. As he looked down the hill through the shade of the trees, he realized that he was the only person in town who had anything left. All the people who were wealthy had lost most of their belongings in the flood. He felt grateful for the first time in his life for what he had. It was a shame that it took all this for him to realize this. As he thought of what was happening in his life, he realized that the entire time he thought his life was terrible, in all actuality, God was taking care of him and molding him to prepare him for better things. What Thomas didn't realize was that God was also preparing him for far more difficult times than he had ever imagined.

Thomas and Emily were married by Mr. Krauss at the little white church that sat up on the hill. It was a quaint wedding, but to Thomas, it was the most beautiful scene he had ever seen. White roses lined the pews, and white wax candles were placed in each window. Emily wore her mother's wedding dress. Her beautiful blonde hair was pulled up as she walked down the aisle. The candles in the room danced in her beautiful green eyes as Mr. Krauss stopped in front of Thomas.

Mr. Avery was Thomas's best man. "She's gorgeous," he whispered into Thomas's ear

"She is." Thomas basked in the moment as his dreams came true in that moment. All he had ever hoped for was now a reality.

In the days that followed, Thomas and Emily enjoyed every moment with each other. They knew their time of enjoyment would soon come to an end, and Thomas would have to leave. It was surreal. It was a happy time but also a sad one because they both knew what was coming. When the time come, Mr. and Mrs. Krauss, along with Mr. Avery, walked with Thomas to the bus stop. They said their goodbyes and left Thomas and Emily to be alone.

Thomas ran his hands on Emily's cheeks as tears rolled down and dripped off her chin. Thomas couldn't hold his back either.

"I don't want you to go." Emily lay her forehead on Thomas's chest.

Thomas looked up into the sky. The sky was blue, and there was a slight breeze in the air. The summer sun was setting and lit up the clouds a peach color as the crickets chirped in the distance. "I'll be back before you know it." Thomas had a peculiar feeling in his heart as those words left his mouth. It was a feeling as though when he returned, things wouldn't be the same. The feeling, though, was not one of dread but of peace. He looked back into her eyes. "You take care of yourself while I'm gone so that baby will be healthy."

Emily nodded and wiped the tears from her eyes. "You know I will."

In the distance, Thomas heard the growl of an engine, and the headlights of a bus soon reached them.

Emily squeezed Thomas tightly. "Whenever you miss me, just look up at those crosses on that hillside and know God's with you—and with me."

Thomas pulled out his mother's journal out of his bag. "I want to give this to you." Thomas handed Emily the journal. "This was my mother's. When I read this, I always feel at peace. I think that you should have it."

Emily nodded and gave Thomas a kiss.

"I love you, Emily." Thomas stepped onto the bus and took a seat at the front. The doors shut, and he watched Emily wave through the window as she soon disappeared into the distance.

CHAPTER 7

Transformation

Thomas walked in the processing center. The floors were shinning and the walls bright white. It was cool inside the building. Thomas was thankful to be out of the heat. He had slept all night outside on the pavement, and it was already hot when the sun came up. He was also very thirsty. Thomas wasn't nervous about being in the military. In fact, the realization he was soon going to war hadn't hit him yet. Nothing seemed real to him. It was more like a dream. He knew nothing about the military or what it consisted of. All he knew was they carried guns and wore a uniform. Thomas had no idea that his life was about to change drastically, and everything he knew would be thrown out the window.

Thomas went to the front desk. There a woman sat typing on a typewriter. Her lips were pursed and her eyes squinty. She looked very unfriendly, but Thomas thought she would know where he needed to go. "Ma'am, I was wondering where I need to go to sign in?"

The woman looked up from her typing. She sighed and looked up at Thomas slowly. Then she looked back down at her typewriter and continued typing.

"Ma'am. Could you please help me? I've come a long ways."

"You see those seats over there? Go take your butt and park it in one of them. I'll be with you when I'm finished," the woman replied.

Thomas didn't much like people speaking to him this way. He thought about telling the woman how rude she was but thought otherwise. About an hour later, Thomas was awakened by a loud thud. The woman from the desk was standing over him.

"Sir, I need to see your call-to-duty slip. I think you're in the wrong place because our next group of individuals aren't supposed to show up for another couple weeks," she said.

"Yes, ma'am, here is my slip," Thomas replied.

She took the slip over to the typewriter. She typed on the typewriter for a few minutes and then went through a door next to her desk. Thomas could hear her talking to someone inside. She was only in there for a couple minutes before she finally came out. Thomas sat waiting patiently looking at all the posters on the walls. They were war posters from the Korean conflict and World War II. The men in the photographs seemed like superheroes. They were muscular and square-jawed. Their uniforms were equivalent to Superman's, and they all were courageous. Thomas felt like he could not be like the men in these posters. He was a scrawny uneducated country boy. He could barely do a push-up. He suddenly wanted to be back home. He realized this wasn't the place for him. He wasn't meant to fight in a war. He didn't even understand what Vietnam was about. The term *communism* was just as foreign as the Spanish language.

Just as his thoughts began to bother him, the woman came abruptly out of the office. "Mr. Bailey, you need to come in here. There seems to be an issue with your paperwork. We can't find the Navy's message for you. It seems that whoever wrote this message to you accidentally put the Navy as the sender."

Thomas was confused. Did this mean he could go home? He hoped that it had been a mistake that they even contacted him. Thomas slowly walked into the doorway beside the woman's desk. The room was dim and smelled of vanilla pipe smoke. Thomas thought of his cigarettes and that he wouldn't mind having a puff off that pipe since it had been a couple days since his last cigarette.

"Son, you better pop to attention when you enter my quarters," Thomas heard as he walked through the doorway. There was a man sitting in the corner. He was an older man whose face looked as evil as any man Thomas had ever seen. His yellow teeth clenched a black pipe in between them, and his eyes were as black as the mines

Thomas had worked in. "You hear me, skinny? Pop to attention!" the man yelled.

Thomas was suddenly nervous. This man had taken him off guard. He was frightening. On second thought, maybe he didn't want a puff from that pipe. Thomas didn't know what standing at attention meant, so he saluted the crusty old man who was screaming at him from the corner of the room. The old man chuckled. Then his chuckle became a hysterical laugh. His laugh reminded Thomas of what Santa's laugh might be like if he existed—minus the fact that this man was much more terrifying than the image of Santa Claus.

"Boy, you have a lot to learn, son. You're as pitiful as that puppy I ran over this morning pulling out of my driveway."

Thomas felt a large lump develop in his throat.

"Son, you had better get your mind r—"

The man was abruptly interrupted by the woman from the front desk. "Sergeant First Class Grey, this is Thomas Bailey. Mr. Bailey, this is Sergeant First Class Grey."

"Pleased to meet you, Mr. Grey," Thomas said.

"My name is not 'Mr. Grey,' son. It's *First Sergeant* Grey. I work for a living. Now sit your butt down in one of those chairs and keep your eyes off me. We need to make a phone call to see where you are supposed to be. I sure hope they tell me you're a puddle pirate because I can't stand the thought of a scrawny body like you being in my army."

Thomas slowly sat down and stared at the wall. Normally, this type of language from another person would make Thomas angry, but it was intimidating coming from this crusty old man. His voice seemed to exhaust authority. Every word was like a king's command. First Sergeant Grey got on his telephone and spun the numbers until he let out a puff of smoke and brought his fingers up to his pipe to start the next inhale.

"Sir, I have a Thomas Bailey here with a letter stating he was drafted and was to report here in two weeks. Yes, sir, two weeks. I'm not sure why he is so early, sir. Yes, sir, better early than late. No, sir, he's a scrawny body. Yes, sir, I will hold." First Sergeant's eyes left the desk and focused on Thomas. He looked Thomas up and down. "Let me see those hands, boy," First Sergeant commanded.

Thomas stuck his hands out. First Sergeant grabbed both of Thomas's hands and jerked Thomas. First Sergeant inspected Thomas's hands closely as if he were reading a map, trying to find the right direction to go in. He took another puff of smoke and blew it in Thomas's face. "So it looks as if you've actually crawled off your mama's lap and did some work in your life. I like that, son. You might be scrawny, but at least you're not worthless."

First Sergeant redirected his attention to the phone. "Yes, sir, I am still here. Oh, really? I wasn't aware of such a situation. Yes, sir. I will take care of it. Thank you, sir."

First Sergeant took the phone and placed it slowly back on the receiver. "Well, son, seeing as how you came here two weeks early and the fact that we have nowhere for you, and also the fact that nearly a thousand United States soldiers have died in the past week, you have been reassigned to the Army, and effective immediately, you are to report to Fort Knox, Kentucky, tomorrow morning. Welcome on, son. Now get out of my office!"

That night, Thomas boarded a bus. It was filled with young men, all of whom didn't say a word. Thomas found the first empty seat he could find. Thomas put his things under his seat and looked up. Everyone was looking straight ahead, not saying a word. Thomas looked to his right. There sat the boy who tormented him nearly his entire life. It was Zack Linsey. Zack was a strong boy growing up. He was the son of a lawyer and always had the best clothes and nice things. He always gave Thomas a beating any chance he could. Thomas was afraid of Zack all his life. Thomas suddenly felt fear. He didn't want to suffer though Zack's beatings on a daily basis. Zack hadn't noticed him. Maybe he could grab his things and head toward the back of the bus, but his thought was too late.

Zack slowly turned to his left. "Well, if it isn't my little whipping boy," Zack said with a grimace replacing the stern look upon his face.

"Ay! Does this look like a social club to you? Do you want me to stick my foot up your hind end? No, you don't! I don't, and nobody else does, because I'd lose my boot, and if I lose my boot because of one of you two, everyone will pay the price, so be quiet and face forward and keep your big mouths shut!" someone from the back of the bus yelled.

Thomas didn't dare look back. He was afraid of what type of beast may be lurking back there. The bus ride was long. Time seemed to stand still. With every telephone pole they passed, the more dread set in on Thomas. The ride was lonely. Passing all these seemingly endless pastures and woodlands seemed to put Thomas back in a state of darkness. It began to rain, and Thomas thought about what Emily must be doing on a day like today. She would always sit on her front porch and bring out a pitcher of sweet tea and bring a blanket outside to cuddle up on her porch swing. Thomas loved to watch her just stare out at the field with a happy look on her face. Her sweet olive skin looked so pure. He always wondered what it was she was dreaming about. He always wished that it was him she was dreaming about. She was the most beautiful thing he had ever seen.

"Everybody up off their rears and off the bus!" the man from the back of the bus screamed.

Thomas had fallen asleep dreaming of Emily and awoke to the sound of panic and screaming. Everyone was pushing one another to get off the bus, and Thomas was shoved toward the front. He exited the bus. There, waiting for him, were four men of brute stature all wearing uniforms that appeared to be chiseled out of stone. All were clean-shaven, and all looked like they could piss fire.

"Everyone get in a line, smallest in front to tallest in the back!" one man yelled.

In the ensuing months that followed, Thomas learned a lot about himself. When everyone else seemed to be mentally breaking down, Thomas felt normal. He would hear men crying at night. They would talk about how they missed their families and their wives. Most of the men were guys who didn't have any education. One who particularly suffered was his good buddy Zack. Soon Thomas realized why he was having an easier time than everyone else. Thomas had suffered mentally his whole life. He had been the provider for his family since he was thirteen years old. Most of these men had never been on their own.

A few of the colored boys seemed to have an easier time like Thomas did. They were from Mississippi. Thomas had never been around colored folks before. He actually had never seen a colored person all his life except in a magazine once. But oddly they reminded Thomas of the men in the mines. He noticed some of the white men would give them dirty looks, and some would steal from them or manipulate them into getting in trouble at times. Thomas didn't understand why. He thought of how the men were covered in soot when they came from the mines. They were black as midnight, but no one ever bothered them about the color of their skin. Thomas thought hard about this. Was it because they could wash the soot off at the end of the day? Thomas had been abused and picked on all his life. He understood in some ways the way they felt.

Thomas made a choice in boot camp. He decided to turn his attention to his weakness, which was his physical stature. Mentally, he was strong; but physically, he was one of the weakest in his class. So every night after the lights were turned off, Thomas would get out of his bed and do extra push-ups and extra sit-ups. At lunch and dinner, he would eat extra food, if they would allow him. Thomas began to grow in stature at a very rapid pace. By the end of boot camp, Thomas had gained nearly twenty-five pounds. He had never been able to eat three meals a day before he stayed with Mr. Krauss, and he had never been physically active. The army taught him how to build his body and be strong mentally and physically. Thomas excelled in harsh conditions while others fell behind.

At his graduation, Thomas was promoted to Private First Class Bailey. He was very proud of his accomplishment. All the rest of his class had graduated as a private. He especially wanted to see Zack's face when his drill instructors pinned the rank on his shoulder. But Zack had fallen during an exercise and broke his leg. He was later discharged, and Thomas didn't see him again. He wished he was still here to see this. Thomas would go over and tell him, "Private, your shoes need polished." Thomas chuckled in his head. He was to have one week off after his boot camp was finished. Thomas was a new man. He was more disciplined and appreciated things more. He had gained twenty-five pounds of muscle. He also thought about how he missed Emily so much. She was everything to him, so for the week off, Thomas planned to go home and spend it with his family. He could barely wait to see Emily, but he also wondered if Emily would have anything to do with him since he left in such a terrible manner. He was worried but at the same time anxious for what lay ahead. He could barely wait to show up in his new uniform, looking clean and crisp. He was proud of his accomplishments. So as soon as graduation finished, Thomas headed for the exit of Fort Knox and was going to catch the next bus back to Charleston. But it seemed fate had other plans for Thomas. Just as soon as Thomas got to the front gate to leave base, a car pulled up next to him. It was his drill sergeant. "Hop in, Private First Class. Take a ride with me," his drill instructor told him.

"Sir, I'm in a hurry, and I need to catch the next—"

Thomas was cut short, "Get your ass in the car."

"Yes, sir." Thomas climbed in the car.

His drill instructor didn't say anything, and neither did Thomas. Thomas didn't understand what he did wrong, but he wasn't going to question his drill instructor even though he had graduated. He knew better. By the road they were driving on, Thomas knew that they were headed to the general's quarters. They ran this route every day for physical training, and he knew that only one person lived down this street: it was the general. Thomas suddenly got nervous. He wasn't sure why his drill instructor would take him down this road unless there was something wrong.

Soon they reached the general's quarters. His home was white with pillars. The American flag flew in front of his home, and closely underneath was the army's flag. The grass was cut and pristine, and there was not a blemish on the whole lot. Thomas was afraid to walk on his grass for leaving one of the perfect blades bent. But then again, he wasn't supposed to walk on the grass anyway. So up the concrete they walked toward the big white door. Thomas's drill instructor knocked three times on the door and stood at attention, as did Thomas. The door was answered by a beautiful woman. She was tall and slender. Her eyes were blue, and her lipstick was ruby red. She looked as clean and spotless. She fit well with the house and grass.

"Good morning, ma'am. We are here to report to General Brantley," Thomas's instructor said.

"Come in, boys. He will be with you shortly."

Thomas couldn't believe he was setting foot in the general's quarters. Inside was a magnificent display of war memorabilia, and the floors were polished white marble. The furniture looked like it just came out of the plastic. Thomas had never been inside a place this pristine in all his life. It was foreign to him. He wondered how someone could live in a place like this without fear of getting something dirty. Just then, the general came down the beautiful winding staircase. He was wearing his uniform and had a very serious look on his face.

"Ah, gentleman, so good to see the both of you. As you can guess, I don't get too many visitors here. One, it is against tradition, and two, I am never home. But let's get down to business. The reason I brought you here, Private First Class Bailey, was to ask you to do something for me," the general said.

"Yes, sir, what can I do for you?" Thomas replied.

"I would like for you to try out for a team, Private First Class. The team is an exceptional group of soldiers. Their training is rigorous, and most individuals do not complete it. You graduated at the top of your class. You are highly motivated, and your drill instructors informed me that when the other men were struggling, you seemed to sail smoothly through. This is a quality that not many soldiers have. That is what we are looking for in a Green Beret soldier. This war's intensity is increasing. The Vietcong are fighting a guerilla war in Vietnam, Thomas. This means we need more guerilla-style soldiers to fight the Vietcong."

Thomas had no idea what a Green Beret was, but he had overheard some of the other guys in his class mention that they would like to be a Green Beret soldier. "Sir, I'm not sure what a Green Beret soldier is," Thomas replied.

"Well, son, I can tell you this. They are an elite fighting force, and not many men can be a Green Beret. They fight when no one else can or will. It takes a special individual to do it, and you are special, Thomas. You just have to give it a try and see if my analysis of you is actually the truth."

"I'll give it a shot, sir," replied Thomas.

* * * * *

Thomas trained for months with the Green Beret. His training nearly broke him. His suffering in life was nothing compared to the conditions and training of the Green Berets, but Thomas soon found out his harsh upbringing not only helped him suffer less, but it actually made him a leader. It pushed him on the inside and physically. He helped the other recruits by pushing them through and helped them to learn to deal with their pain by releasing it in their training exercises. In his training, Thomas made some good friends, but one in particular he grew very close to. There was a Hispanic man named Javier in Thomas's class. Although he was Hispanic—and sometimes the men would give him a hard time—he had the respect of the entire class because he was a medic. Everybody just called him Doc. That was a lot easier than *Javier* and, within the ranks, a lot more respectable.

Thomas and Doc grew close because both were from small town, and both got teased a little. Thomas wasn't teased for his ethnicity but for his accent and where he was from. Thomas gained the nickname "Hillbilly" by the end of training, although his comrades respected him and his mental strength. The training that the men received was tough. Most men couldn't withstand the training and dropped out. During the extensive training, Thomas had noticed that every night or before each exercise, Doc would bow on one knee and pray. Thomas didn't mention it to Doc, but he wondered why he would pray. Thomas was skeptical of prayer and God, but Doc always seemed to have a good attitude even when the training seemed to suck the spirit right out of everyone else.

One day after a miserable training exercise, Thomas looked over to see Doc smiling. Thomas could barely stand and was in physical misery. His feet were blistered and wet from sweat. His curiosity got the better of him, and he walked over to where Doc sat.

"Say, you look awfully happy to have went through all that."

Doc smiled at Thomas and laughed a little.

"So what's the secret to your happiness in this God-awful mess we're involved with?" Thomas asked, panting. A few of the other men looked at Doc and waited on his reply.

Doc's smile faded slightly, and he answered, "The mind sometimes becomes weak. The body usually follows. Humans in general become weak when they are faced with obstacles. One thing I have learned through my faith is even when your strength mentally and physically becomes weak, the strength of your spirit is something that will never give up or tire out on you—that is, if your spirit is in the right place." Doc looked at Thomas and smiled again. "Jesus can give you an undefeated and unbeatable spirit."

A few of the men laughed. "You're crazy, Doc," one of the men said.

Thomas looked at Doc and could see in his eyes that he was serious. He had this peculiar thing about him that Thomas just couldn't put a finger on. It made Thomas a little uncomfortable sometimes, but it was his own insecurity that caused these feelings. Thomas just brushed it off and grabbed Doc's shoulder. "Well, hopefully that spirit will rub off on me because I'm wore out and want to go home!" Thomas said jokingly.

All the men verbally agreed and laughed.

* * * * *

Thomas lay in his cot that night and stared at the sky. The summer heat had just started to cool off, and it was comfortable in the field. Doc sat beside him on his own cot quietly, reading a Bible. Thomas looked over at Doc and saw him reading. "Can I ask you a question, Doc?"

"Ask away, my friend," Doc replied as he closed his Bible.

"Those comments you made today about your spirit staying strong—do you think that anyone can feel that inside them no matter how hard they are inside?"

Doc pursed his lips. "Well, maybe." Doc turned to face Thomas. "When I was growing up, I had four brothers and two sisters. I was the second youngest. We had a good relationship among one another all my life. One day, my father came home and told us that he lost his job. Then everything changed. My mother went to work at a flour mill making two dollars an hour, and my father, being as old as he was, couldn't find anyone who would give him a job. The food portions got smaller and smaller until we struggled to get a meal every couple days. Nine people are a lot to feed, you know?"

Doc lowered his head. "After almost a year and a half, my mother became ill. She passed away not even three months later. My father followed, along with three of my brothers. My sisters, along with my brother, tried to find whatever they could to bring food home, but unfortunately, the only thing left was selling drugs. My brother pushed while my sisters sold the drugs. A lot of the time, the buyers wanted to sample the dope, so they asked my sisters to use. It was basically a test to see if they were selling straight product or trying to rip them off. One of my sisters became an addict. The other turned to prostitution."

Thomas could see a tear flowing down Doc's cheek.

"I saw what happened to them, and I didn't want to be a part of that. I figured the only way I could escape was to leave Cuba and try to make it to the United States. I found a few people who knew a man who would take people halfway and then give them a raft to float the rest of the way to Florida. It was a long shot that anyone live, but I figured it was worth the risk to make it here to the United States. It was a better option than dying like my family. One day out to sea, a storm hit. Our raft was tossed all over. Everyone was scared, except one old lady on the raft. I was just a kid, but I remember what she said to me. She looked right into my eyes and said, 'The Lord is my light and my salvation—whom shall I fear? The Lord is the stronghold of my life—of whom shall I be afraid?'" Doc stopped his story and looked toward the sky. "It's a beautiful night, isn't it, hillbilly?" Doc looked back down at Thomas with a smile.

Thomas was astounded. All this time, he had thought his life was tough. *There is always someone going through far worse.* "It sure is, Javier."

By the end of the extensive training, Thomas had gained fifteen more pounds. His class had the largest success rate of any Green Beret class in history. This was mainly due to the men within the company and the bonds between the men. Thomas was no longer physically a small man. He would be unrecognizable to the young man who hopped on the bus to head toward Charleston. But all the while, Thomas was missing home and, most of all, Emily. It had been almost a year since he had seen Emily. He had written her a couple letters, but it was hard trying to squeeze anything in with the grueling training. It would be just a few days before their child was due. Thomas couldn't wait to go home for a couple weeks and spend all his time with Emily, and he was so excited to meet his child. As he talked with his fellow soldiers after graduation, their commander made an unexpected visit to the podium.

"Wonder what this is about?" one of the men asked.

"I don't know, but it's probably not good." Thomas could see the uneasy look on the commander's face.

The men all stood at attention as the commander took the stage. "At ease, gentlemen," the commander quietly said into the microphone. The commander cleared his throat. "As you all are aware, most graduating classes are awarded two weeks of rest and relaxation after they complete their training. I know this journey has not been an easy one, and it takes a special man to be a Green Beret." The commander's sentence was silenced as he looked down at his notes. "I regret to inform you all that the entire graduating class will leave tomorrow morning and head for Thailand, where you will meet your respective platoon leaders. I know this is a disappointment, but the fighting in Vietnam has escalated, and we are in dire need for more guerilla-style fighters in Vietnam. You guys are basically all that stand in the way of the NVA boys. I wish you all luck, and may God watch over you."

Thomas watched as the commander stepped away from the podium. The air was still. Confusion seemed to sweep over everyone, and then the realization came that nobody would get to see their families before they left for Vietnam. Most would never see their families again. Doc placed his hand on Thomas's shoulder. He didn't say anything, but Thomas thought about Doc's situation. He wouldn't get to see his family even if they would have given them rest and relaxation time. Thomas had to get to a phone before he left to let Emily know what was happening. Thomas was so angry and so sad at the same time. He would miss the birth of his only child.

CHAPTER 8

Coming to Grips

As Thomas sat in the cargo plane, the loud hum of the engines were drowned out by his thoughts of home and Emily. He tried to imagine what the baby must look like. Thomas pictured a child who looked like Emily looking up at him with her big green eyes. Thomas knew no matter what, she was beautiful. His heart was swollen, and it was hard to think about home and the people he loved. The more he thought, the more his heart fell to pieces. To take the attention off his aching chest, he changed his focus to where he was heading and tried his best to mentally prepare for what lay ahead of him. If he wanted to make it back, he had to focus.

In training, his instructors educated him in the Vietnamese culture. Vietnam was a third world county. Its people were traditional, and its soldiers from the north wore no specific uniform. They didn't use rules when they fought, and they did not have mercy for those whom they caught. They believed in what they were fighting for. It was their land and their people. But America, knowing what freedom feels like, wanted to keep communist ideas from spreading, and the south wanted democracy. Thomas, though, had no feelings toward the country or political agendas. He was a soldier. It was his job to do what his superiors told him and, most importantly, survive. Thomas just wanted to go home, and he was going to do whatever it took to make it back. His feelings, though, had not yet worn the burdens of war. His hands were still clean and his soul intact. Determination had become his motivation.

One thing Thomas's training could never prepare him for, however, was that Vietnam was an untamed beast and the closest thing to hell a man could get on this earth. Reality was creeping around the corner, and Thomas had his back turned. All of America did. Thomas was first flown to Germany and then to Thailand, where he traveled by vehicle to Cambodia to the city of Phnom Penh. Peace was still intact when his feet left the ground, and that would be the last day of Thomas's time in Vietnam that peace would be felt. Thomas arrived by way of an AH-1 Cobra. The blades whooped and seemed to send a pulse through your bones. The sand made your teeth gritty, and it took a week to wash out the particles from places the sun didn't shine.

As the chopper left the ground, Thomas got a first look at how unstable and treacherous this battle would be. Thomas first flew southeast to Ho Chi Minh City, or as we best know it, Saigon. The entire trip, the sound of stray bullets could be heard pinging off the metal of the choppers. Thomas began to realize how real death was in this place. You had to be aware of everything around you in order to survive, and sometimes that wouldn't even help you live. The enemy was all around and, in some cases, even underneath you. Hours after takeoff, Thomas finally reached Saigon. He couldn't wait to get his feet on the ground. At least then he could run or hide or even shoot back. His mission was clear. He was first to meet his fellow Green Berets in Bien Hoa; then they were to fly to Gia Lai, where they were to hold the area from the incoming NVA. The NVA were the ground forces fighting for the Vietnam People's Army. They were the communists from Northern Vietnam. They were sided with the Viet Cong, who were southern communists from Southern Vietnam. Both the NVA and the Viet Cong were supported by China, the Soviet Union, North Korea, Cuba, Czechoslovakia, Burma, and Bulgaria. The goal was to meet the First Cavalry, who were already there and waiting on the go-ahead to advance on the enemy. Thomas was to be among the first to see the tip of the NVA's spear. He just didn't know it.

It was a dry day. Usually, Vietnam was humid and damp, and sometimes it would rain for months with no end in sight. Today was different. It was dry and dusty. The sun shone heavily above, and sweat poured from Thomas's body. There was no way of cooling off. The heat was just something you had to deal with. Thomas finally arrived in Ia Drang at the break of dawn. When he arrived, soldiers were preparing their weapons, and silence had swept over the camp like a blanket of dread. Thomas knew battle was coming. No man kept quiet like this unless death was waiting, so he knew he shouldn't waste time.

He and his fellow Green Berets went straight to the commanding officer to gather the information they needed in order to assess the enemy. However, their plans were cut short. Intel had just received a message: there were approximately two hundred NVA soldiers in the Chu Pong Mountains, and First Cavalry was to advance with their four hundred soldiers. They were to fly in on choppers and meet the enemy after all the choppers had landed their men in the zone. The only problem was that each chopper could hold six men at a time, and only eight choppers could land in the zone. It would take hours to land four hundred men, and this had everyone worried. What would happen if the NVA were to advance before they could land all their men? This was the First Cavalry's first assault in Vietnam. It had to go smoothly.

Thomas and the Green Berets decided to split up and go in with the cavalry units. They wanted a piece of the NVA. Around 10:30 a.m., the first choppers took off from the ground. It was thirteen minutes to the landing zone. In order to keep the NVA from advancing, Firebase Falcon would shell artillery into the NVA front lines to allow the choppers to land. They were to cease fire one minute in advance to the choppers dropping the first units of the battalion off. If they stopped just a minute too soon, the NVA could advance and kill all the soldiers who were dropped off first before the other soldiers could make it into the landing zone on their choppers. Another worry was that they wouldn't stop soon enough, and their artillery rounds would rain down upon the choppers. Everything had to go perfectly.

Thomas was on the fourth helicopter of the first eight. Thomas was a little worried about the timing of the artillery, but he had faith in his fellow soldiers. In his mind, two hundred NVA against one hundred American soldiers was an easy task. This society and its people were uneducated and very incompetent to modern warfare. There was no possibility of them being able to fight against a superpower like the United States. What Thomas didn't know was that sometimes grit outweighs technology and strength, and his confidence blinded him from the very thing he was taught repeatedly never to forget: never underestimate your enemies. Fortunately for the American soldiers, the artillery rounds kept the advancing NVA at bay. Thomas was one of the first to hit the ground, and he was one of the first to see the NVA soldiers. First Cavalry had even caught a prisoner of war.

As Thomas looked at the NVA soldier, it supported his theory that the NVA were weak and unprepared. The NVA soldier had rags for clothes. He had no shoes and barely stood five feet tall. He must have barely weighed one hundred pounds. Thomas chuckled on the inside. He might make it out alive, after all, he thought. Thomas took his gear off and sorted the things he was going to bring with him. This would surely be a quick fight, so he wouldn't need an extra canteen, and he left his knife as well. With Firebase Falcon shelling artillery, he didn't expect to face the enemy at a close range. Thomas relaxed his mind to the thought of death. He now had hope that this would be a short and easy battle. But his thoughts were interrupted by his first lieutenant.

"Three damn battalions! That little bastard said that there are three damn battalions up on that hillside! And to top it off, they're scratching their butts and gritting their teeth to put a round of lead in each of our heads!"

Thomas was confused. *Three battalions?* That was over 1,600 men. There were only supposed to be 200. "But, sir, we don't have all our men here yet. There are barely two hundred that have landed. We're outnumbered eight to one, sir."

"That's good math, Bailey, but I don't think the NVA are afraid they may offend us by not waiting on the other two hundred men to land before they pour off that hillside and shell our asses. Get your shit set up. I don't know about you, but if I'm going to die, I'm going to die fighting, and I'm going to kill as many of those sons of bitches I can."

Thomas suddenly realized that now the tables had turned. They were outnumbered eight to one. Suddenly the enemy and threat of these people became real to Thomas. *I could die today.* It would take a miracle to live through this, but Thomas had little faith of a miracle and less faith that the remaining two hundred troops would make it here before the NVA reached the landing zone from the mountains ahead. They had the high ground. That was a serious problem.

Forty-four minutes had passed. Everything had been quiet up to this point. Thomas found himself belly down in a ditch that looked into the mountains above. There had been no sign of the NVA advancing. Choppers continued to come in but at a slow pace. He was sweating, and his fingers were slipping on the grip of his gun, and his sweat made his eyes burn. He sat, afraid to take a breath too loud. The jungle ahead looked dark and alive. It was as if he was looking into something that held an animal. It was an animal that was ready to kill him. It was waiting on the right moment for Thomas to take his eyes off it so it could claim its prey. Thomas's mouth was dry. He could barely breathe without licking his lips. His eyes burned. He didn't want to blink. He just wanted to survive.

In his worry, Thomas thought about how he wanted to be home. He thought of how this all started. He thought he could handle death and was ready for it. But his memories of Emily and his daughter he had not yet met filled his chest with fire. What if he could never go home again? What if he died today and he would never see Emily again? Thomas's thoughts were interrupted by a hiss. Then another hiss that seemed to pass right by his ear. Silence was broken by the deafening sound of gunfire all around him. Thomas was frozen. This was something he couldn't foresee or comprehend. This noise shattered him. Thomas looked all around. Everyone was screaming. Men were lying bleeding, limbs missing, and some he could not recognize. Their faces were gone, just bodies of men implanted into a nightmare Thomas was living. No face to go with their name tags on their uniforms.

Thomas turned to face the cloud of NVA. He could not see anything. The air was filled with smoke, and the smell of gunpowder from the casings of bullets burned his nostrils. His face got hot, and his body stiffened. Suddenly Thomas felt something hot on his shoulder. The burn became immediately overwhelmingly painful. Thomas reached up to try and get rid of whatever was burning his shoulder, but nothing was there. Thomas's hand felt wet. He looked at it. It was red. It was blood. Reality finally came to Thomas. He had been grazed by a bullet in his shoulder. Thomas raised his arm to make sure it still worked. Fear gripped him for the first time. This was reality. What he was experiencing was real. This was no dream. The pain, the chaos—everything was real.

Thomas's mind snapped back into his head, and he regained his sense of awareness. He grabbed his rifle and placed it on his shoulder. All the pain he had felt growing up and all the trials and tribulations he experienced came into his mind. The pain of working day in and day out to support his dying mother and feeling alone all those years flashed visions in his head. The pain he allowed his father to bestow upon him and of his training and the months he weathered through with the memory Emily all flooded his mind at the same time. Then something happened inside of Thomas. It was as if a beast had awakened inside of him. Thomas stood up. He could hear bullets sizzling by his head, but he no longer saw them as something to fear. Thomas's mind expanded to the realization that all his pain was for a reason. All the darkness and struggle was for a purpose. All the days of his feet hurting from the rock and the scabs from his knees scraping the black rocks of the mines were for a reason. The crawling and agony of his soul bleeding had all been for a bigger purpose. Thomas realized that in this moment, God had answered the question Thomas had asked so long ago—*why?* Why had his life been so terrible? Why had he been beat down to nothingness and continued on? It was for this day. It was to prepare him to survive so he could make it back to the one good thing he had in his life. It was to bring him back to Emily.

I'm not going to die on this day for anyone!

Things here didn't seem bad to Thomas anymore. It was here Thomas knew he was supposed to be. The darkness he had felt had surrounded him in this jungle. He was immune to it. All the cries of men dying and the chaos were something Thomas was used to. These were the cries of his soul. Now it was heard with his ears instead of his heart. He was used to pain and tribulation. But now he could fight back. Now he could unleash what he kept inside. The beast he kept inside had been chained up, and Thomas knew his reason for being here was to unleash it so he might live. God had made him suffer to numb him to the hell that was surrounding him. It was to get him out of this jungle alive and back to Emily. Thomas finally understood.

Thomas closed one eye and looked down the barrel of his weapon. It became an extension of his body. NVA scurried in his line of sight like rats in a corn barn. *Tat! Tat-tat-tat* Thomas's finger seemed to have a mind of its own. Every NVA who scurried out of the trees were met with hot lead in the face. One by one, the small men Thomas met began to stack up like fire kindling. Thomas crawled on his knees. They were hardened from the countless hours he spent on them in the mines. He crawled on his belly, scratching his hands and legs and shoulders, yet he felt none of it as he passed over the bodies of the dead. His main focus was survival. But in his quest for bloodshed, Thomas didn't expect to have someone else depending on him. While crawling through the jungle and under heavy fire, Thomas came across three other US soldiers who were pinned down by enemy fire. Two were wounded, and the other was a familiar face.

"Thomas, is that you, buddy?"

"Tray! Where is the rest of our platoon?"

"I don't know!" Tray screamed. The deafening sounds of gunfire and explosions vibrated the ground beneath Thomas's feet. "We need to try and find Doc!" Thomas pulled a grenade from his pouch, pulled the pin, and then hurled it in the direction of the machine-gun fire. There was a loud boom and then silence in the vicinity.

"I think you got 'em, Thomas!" Tray screamed. He didn't realize how loud he was because his ears were ringing.

Thomas's goal was to cut off the NVA from the side and give the three men cover while they slipped out of the area. Thomas slowly crawled about sixty yards before he reached the enemy line.

There he saw an enemy soldier by himself. He was a sniper. He was well camouflaged. Thomas nearly crawled right on top of him as he was so well hidden. Thomas thought about shooting him, but the NVA might recognize the gunfire from behind them, and this would eliminate the element of surprise. So Thomas pulled out his knife from its sheath and inched closer to the sniper. He reared back his knife, preparing to thrust it into the back of the sniper's neck when he heard a yell from behind him. Thomas bad been spotted by the sniper's spotter. He had been lagging behind for some reason.

Thomas quickly rolled over on his back as the tiny NVA soldier ran toward him. Thomas noticed the sniper had turned to see what was happening as well. Both of the NVA soldiers came down on Thomas. Thomas grabbed one man by the throat and the other by his hand. A large buoy knife was in the sniper's grasp. Thomas did what any man would do in a life-or-death situation: he did what it took to live. Thomas sank his teeth into the sniper's cheek and bit down as hard as he could. A metallic taste filled his mouth as the sniper began to scream. Thomas pulled away, still holding on to the man's cheek with his teeth. The NVA soldier yelped in pain. Thomas then dug his fingernail into the other NVA soldier's throat. He pressed as hard as he could until he felt the man's windpipe crunch. He threw the dead NVA soldier off him and focused on the sniper, whom he still had yelping by his teeth. He wrapped both his hands around the back of his neck and released his bite, then thrust his knee as hard upward as he could while pulling the man down. Thomas's knee sank into the side of the man's head, knocking him out.

Thomas fell backward. His stomach felt sick. He quickly spat all the blood in his mouth out and wiped it off him. He felt disgusted. Even though it was the only thing he could do to stay alive, his soul felt violated in a way. He quickly grabbed the sniper's knife and stabbed the NVA soldier in the chest. Thomas was tired and beat up, but this was not the first time he had been in pain and left for dead. His mind went back to the winter night he was left in the street to freeze to death, but God had found a way for him to live by sending the shooting star to direct his attention to the nativity scene.

Thomas realized that God had been watching out for him all along at this moment of chaos. He just didn't realize it.

Thomas gathered his feelings and eased his way down the enemy line, killing the NVA soldiers one by one. He found a violin chord in the sniper's knapsack. It was used to sneak up behind his enemies and thrust around their neck until it suffocated them to death. Thomas used this to his advantage. He killed each soldier he met with ease using the guitar chord. He had finally reached his way to the center of the enemy's line. This would give the pinned-down American soldiers enough time to get the wounded off the battlefield. Thomas lay on his belly. He was waiting to see if any NVA soldiers came to the front. He expected them to come and aid the line that was failing, but no one did. Thomas decided to head back toward base camp and see if there were any more NVA advancing on the opposite side of the line.

Thomas crept his way back to the American side of the battle front. There were the three men Thomas had seen earlier. "It's safe now to advance on this side of the line. Doc, you need to come this way. I saw a lot of wounded toward the center of the advancing line. They had a machine gun in a nest up there," Thomas said.

The three men looked at Thomas in horror. Shock and disbelief coated their faces.

"Hey, you hear what I said?"

They all shook their heads. "Are you all right?" Doc said quietly.

"I'm fine, but we need to get you toward the center of the line, Doc. There are men everywhere down there that are injured."

Unbeknownst to Thomas, he was unrecognizable as a human being. The blood and dirt had covered him, and the only aspect left unblemished were the whites of his eyes. Doc followed Thomas toward the center of the battle where the American troops had taken heavy machine-gun fire. Bodies lay scattered everywhere. The NVA were still shooting, but the heavy fire had subsided. Thomas and the medic got to the center line. There were heavy American casualties in the area. Dead NVA lay on the battlefield as well. The NVA were advancing off the mountainside, and there was no possibility that the First Cavalry was going to hold off the incoming one thousand or so

NVA left in the area. They were taking heavy fire toward the right flank of the line and were regrouping for an all-out assault on the Americans' weak points in the line. Thomas headed toward the left flank of the battlefield. He didn't get far when a mortar round landed just a few feet from him. The blast knocked Thomas from his feet.

"Hey! Get up!"

Thomas's vision cleared to see Doc's gnarled face screaming just inches from his. There were tiny pieces of shrapnel sticking in his cheekbone, and blood was oozing out of a gash just over his left eye.

"Get up, Tom! We're going to get killed! We're sitting ducks!"

Thomas got up off the jungle canopy. He had a deafening ring in his ear, and he couldn't catch his balance. His vision in his right eye was gone. He reached up to feel for his eyeball. His hand was shaking uncontrollably. He couldn't feel his fingers. Thomas looked down at his hand to see that three of his fingers had been blown off.

"Doc, my hand…" Thomas looked at Doc as bullets zipped by his ears, spraying the trees above and beside him.

"I know, buddy. Don't worry about your hand. It'll be all right!" Doc screamed as dirt spit up all around the three of them. "We're gonna get killed if we don't get out of here!"

Thomas's consciousness came back within him as a bullet grazed the top of his shoulder. It shocked Thomas and sent him back to the ground. Thomas got to his knees and crawled over to Tray. He grabbed his shoulders and dragged him behind a tree. Tray's legs were useless. He had taken multiple gunshots to his knees and thighs, and blood was spurting out of one hole every time his heart took a beat. Thomas looked at him with sweat and blood dripping off his chin.

"Tray, this is going to hurt real bad, buddy. Look at me!"

"Thomas, am I going to die?" Tray said with what little breath he could squeeze out.

"No, buddy, this is just a minor wound. You are going to be okay."

Doc looked at Thomas from a few feet away. Thomas looked at Doc and turned his eyes back to Tray. He was very pale, and his eyes started to roll back in his head. Thomas sank his fingers into the bullet hole and fished around for the artery in Tray's leg. His fingers slipped on and off until finally Thomas was able to pinch off the spewing artery. Tray had taken his bandana off and was screaming into the cloth as Doc finally was able to make his way to them. Thomas looked at Doc as he picked up a handful of mud and stuffed it into the gaping hole on Tray's leg.

"There's no time, Thomas. We've got to get out—"

Doc's sentence was cut short as a bullet passed through his cheekbone.

Blood sprayed on Thomas as Doc fell to the ground. "Doc!" Thomas jumped on Doc, and bullets continued to pass by the three men. Thomas was wounded, but not nearly as bad as Tray or Doc. Thomas looked around as the jungle seemed to quiver with violence. "This is it." He looked around as the whole world seemed to slow down and become quiet. As the NVA ambush enclosed, Thomas's feet began to vibrate, and the earth beneath him shook with force. Just as the feeling of hopelessness consumed him, the rushing NVA were torn to shreds before his very eyes. Each man's body tore to pieces a few feet from Thomas and his wounded brethren. Thomas looked up as bullet casings rained beautifully around him like a metallic spring shower. Backup had arrived, and hell had become impatient as bullets tossed the jungle like a fresh cut salad.

Thomas looked ahead as the last soldier in sight sat on his knees, quivering in pain less than twenty feet from Thomas. The raining jacket casings ceased as the chopper blades slowly faded out of sight, and the jungle was left mutilated. The silence seemed to be more deafening than any other sound Thomas had heard that day. He looked ahead at the small, puny man in front of him. He couldn't be more than one hundred pounds and might stand five feet tall. Thomas looked into the blacks of this man's eyes. Slowly he realized that this was no man. This was just a boy. He probably hadn't even hit puberty yet. He had been shot in the neck, and blood was trickling down his chest as bubbles started to form in another bullet hole just above his sternum.

"Dear God." Tears filled Thomas's eyes. "You're just a boy."

The young Vietnamese boy gasped for air for a few seconds and then collapsed to the jungle floor. Thomas watched as the boy took his last breaths, tears flowing down his face as he grasped Doc's bloody uniform. He wept as the reinforcements swept in around him and created a perimeter surrounding the three men. Two were mortally wounded and the other internally scarred.

The chopper pounded dust all over the bloody men as a medic hopped out and ran toward them. Thomas put his shirt over Doc's face to shield it from the dust.

"Are you three okay?" the medic screamed over the roar of the chopper blades.

"What's it look like?" Doc yelled back.

"Yeah, stupid question. Let's get you guys on this chopper." The medic helped grab Thomas and put him on the plane. Doc started to board. He placed one foot up on the deck and looked up to see the medic's eyes, looking behind him in shock. "RPG!" The plane lifted off the ground and thrust Doc backward onto the dirt. The chopper pulled up, the blades narrowly missing the incoming rocket.

"Doc!" Thomas grabbed the medic's collar. "Hey, where are we going?" Thomas looked into the cockpit.

"Sorry, but it looks like you narrowly missed death. You're going home, buddy." The pilot glanced back at Thomas.

"You're leaving those men down there!"

"I don't have much of a choice. Look down."

Bullets pinged off the side of the chopper as it made a hard left. Thomas looked down to see dozens of NVA soldiers coming out of the trees surrounding the landing zone. Thomas's stomach turned. "Are they sending in reinforcements?"

"They're trying, but they're caught up," the pilot answered.

* * * * *

Doc looked up, trying to see what was happening through all the dust in the air. The chopper was in the distance and going out of sight when gunfire caught his attention. An NVA machine gun was firing from the mountaintop at the chopper, causing it to spiral out of control. He turned the safety off his weapon and headed up the hillside toward the gunfire. Dust blocked most of his sight as the chopper blades and screaming drowned out his thoughts. What was happening was all a reaction. His reaction was dangerous, but death was imminent to all those aboard that chopper, and Doc wasn't going to allow his friend to die.

Tree limbs scraped across his forehead as he ran into the bush, trying to get cover from any NVA that had made their way to the landing zone. The deeper he ran into the jungle, the softer the sound of war was. Soon all he heard was his feet crunching the canopy beneath him and the thud of his heart in his chest. The gunfire had ceased. Doc hadn't noticed in his rush to stop it that all had gone quiet. He stopped and looked for any movement, all the while attempting to control his breathing, which was difficult because of his nerves. He got down and crawled between two tree roots. He sat and listened.

In the distance, he saw four NVA soldiers coming his way. One was carrying the machine gun he had been looking for. Doc knew if he didn't take that gun out, it would mean more innocent lives. He was going to do what he had to do. He placed his sights on the gunner and placed his finger on the trigger. He took a deep breath in, and just as he began to pull the trigger, large movement from the tree line behind the soldiers stopped him. Out of the trees came dozens of soldiers. Too many for Doc to even count. He realized now it wouldn't help to take out the machine gun. He must go and warn the landing zone. He crawled out from under the tree roots and bear-crawled as far as he could, then stood up and took off. Bullets ricocheted off the trees as he passed them. He heard the NVA yelling behind him. Bullets zipped the dirt, and now the only thing that stood in front of the NVA taking over the landing strip was Doc. He ran, close to three to four hundred yards, and finally saw the clearing of the landing zone. American soldiers soon came into view, screaming at him to put his hands up.

"They're coming!" Doc choked out. He could barely breathe. The sheer terror of what was coming frightened him to exhaustion. "They're a couple hundred yards away!"

One soldier ran up to him." How many?"

Doc looked at him, sweat dripping from his forehead and chin. "Hundreds."

"Get that line up here!" The soldier jogged over to the radioman. "Call for backup. We're about to take on an assault we weren't expecting."

Doc looked around at the soldiers. The choppers had just brought a couple dozen more soldiers. They were far outnumbered.

"They're trying to get more guys here right now. That chopper that tried to take off earlier is almost fixed."

Doc's attention was now on the soldier's words. "You said that chopper that was getting shot at is still here?" Doc walked over to the soldier.

"Yeah, you better catch it while you can. You look rough, buddy."

The soldier passed up Doc and began screaming orders. Doc ran over the hump that protected the landing zone from view from the bottom of the mountain. There was Thomas hanging out the side watching the hill intently. Doc saw his friend and started to head toward the chopper when Thomas stood up and screamed, " RPG! RPG!"

Doc turned to see a dozen NVA burst out of the jungle untouched, a soldier in the midst with an RPG strapped over his shoulder. His finger pulled the trigger, and a rocket-propelled grenade came slinging out of the launcher, wildly swaying in every direction but on course in their direction. Doc hit the deck as the grenade hit a group of soldiers behind him. The sound was deafening. The ringing was loud and drowned out all sound that once filled the air. Doc sat up and checked his legs. They were still there. He stood up and looked back at the chopper. The blades were now turning as dirt and dust flew everywhere. The once tallgrass lay flat from the blades pushing them down. There in the chopper at the gun was Thomas. He was screaming at Doc. Doc couldn't hear him. He was waving his arms. Fear was in his eyes, but Doc's consciousness was still in shock from the explosion. He turned around slowly. The sight stunned him into a paralyzed state in which his body couldn't move.

Bullets zipped by Doc as he stood in the open field staring at the dozens of NVA soldiers bombarding the landing zone. Vibrations from explosions shook his feet as he watched dirt spat up all around him from gunfire. He still could not hear anything. It was a quiet chaos that had ensued, and nobody had expected it. Doc's eyes finally moved to the scene surrounding him. American soldiers lay in the grass. Many were wounded by gunshots. Some were missing limbs, and some screamed as others lay quietly.

As Doc took in the scene around him, he felt a tug at his hand. He looked down to see a man with a face full of blood, quivering in pain. Doc realized he was missing an arm. There was a gaping hole in his leg. "Are you a medic?"

Doc couldn't hear him. He stood there looking at the man, not taking into account that his life was in danger by standing in the wide open. The man pulled him down to the ground. Doc's eyes were now ground level. The man screamed into Doc's ears, "Are you a medic!"

Doc could barely hear, but it was loud enough to understand. Reality came to Doc as blood gushed out of the hole in the man's leg. "Yes, I am," he screamed.

"You think you could maybe help me! I'm hurting pretty bad!"

"Yeah, yes, I will help you." Doc looked back to where the chopper sat earlier. It was gone. *Thomas got out of here just in time. Thank goodness.* Doc grabbed the man and dragged him on the ground toward where the landing zone was. NVA scurried past the two men. Doc couldn't believe they didn't see them in the grass. With all his might, he kept going, foot by foot, dragging the man, attempting to make it back to the landing zone where at least they had more cover than in the open field.

Finally, they made it. Doc couldn't feel his arms. They burned, and now his head was pounding from the earlier blast. He lay there, completely exhausted, trying to suck in air. It truly didn't matter what was happening around him. He just breathed. The man whom he dragged was pulled back further by other soldiers as they put a tourniquet around his leg and arm. Doc grabbed his gun and sat up to see what was happening around him. There were explosions all around him. Fire lit up the scene as the scorched earth around him took the place of the once-green rice field.

As he looked around, he noticed that the NVA who had bombarded the area were now gone. Bullets zipped from the tree line of the mountain. *They retreated?* Doc couldn't figure it out. They had overwhelmed them and then withdrew? He kept low, not wanting to get shot. Things soon got quiet, but only for a moment. Doc knew a storm was coming. He could feel it in his gut. The soft and distant whoosh of chopper blades came into his damaged ear as he turned to see the helicopter pass over him just a few feet from his head. The wind shoved him down to the ground. He rolled to his belly and then up to his knees to see the chopper spray the tree line with machine-gun fire and circle back around. The chopper quickly came back into view. There on the gun was his friend Thomas.

The chopper made it back to the landing zone and slowly sank to the ground as soldiers moved in to protect it. Thomas jumped out of the side. The once bright-red blood on his uniform was now dark and dried, and he was limping, but looked determined. "I couldn't leave you, brother."

Doc smiled through the pain. "You are my brother, man." Doc hugged Thomas, and he lifted Doc off the dirt.

"Let's get out of here." The two men stayed low and headed back to the chopper, which was just fifty or so yards from them. "I thought you were dead."

Thomas glanced at Doc. "Not yet."

Doc smirked at Thomas.

"Hey!"

Doc and Thomas stopped to see thee dead NVA lying on the ground in a heap. Doc looked at Thomas. "My mind's playing tricks on me."

"No," Thomas quickly cut him off. He walked over to three heap, his gun pointed at the soldiers. He poked the men to make sure it was no trap and rolled back the NVA soldier on the top. There under him lay an American man. His eyes were on Doc and Thomas. Thomas bent over and grabbed the man's chest and pulled him to his feet. "Let's go."

The three men started to walk when a sudden roar behind them stopped them in their tracks. Doc and Thomas turned slowly to see the tops of the trees at the lower mountain shaking. Thomas turned to Doc. "Run."

Doc didn't understand.

"Run!"

Thomas grabbed Doc's shoulder and pushed him toward the chopper. Doc took one final look back to see what must have been a few hundred NVA running from the tree line. Some carried machine guns. Some had RPGs. The Americans were severely outnumbered. Doc knew this was it. He turned and ran as fast as his legs would carry him. The weight of his gear couldn't even slow him down. The man they had helped was in front of them and soon fell to the ground as a bullet pinged off his helmet. He landed faceup, eyes glazed over. Doc stopped to grab him.

"He's gone! Keep going!"

Doc started again, heading to the back of the landing zone. The chopper's blades were speeding up. He was almost there. Thomas was just about twenty yards ahead of him when a burning sensation filled Doc's abdomen. It stopped him in his tracks. He looked down to see blood oozing from the top of his stomach. He put his hand up to feel the warm flow onto his hand. He looked up at the chopper. Thomas had reached it and was climbing aboard. He turned around to grab Doc as the feet of the bird left the ground.

"Doc! Put this thing back on the ground!" Thomas screamed at the pilot.

"I've got to go now, or we all die!" The pilot pulled back on the grips, and the chopper took off as Doc stood watching in shock.

The NVA was swarming around the landing zone, but the American soldiers, what few there were, fought back for their lives. The first row of NVA fell to the ground as Thomas's arms vibrated from the power of the machine gun. Shell casings flew on his arms, steaming as the hot metal hit his wet arms. He did all he could do. The NVA closed in as the machine gun fired its last bullet.

Out of the trees, a group of NVA emerged, outflanking the Americans. One had an RPG and pointed it to the chopper. But just as the NVA soldier was about to pull the trigger, a bullet passed through his thigh. Doc stood, pistol still pointed in his direction, standing straight up. There was a yell; then a few dozen NVA came from within the bushes running toward Doc. He pulled the trigger on his pistol, but the hammer fell with no discharge and a click to follow. His time had run out, and so had his ammunition.

"You turn this chopper around, or I'll throw you out of that cockpit and fly this thing myself!" Thomas yelled at the pilot.

"You're out of ammunition."

Thomas looked around the cockpit. There, under a dead man, peeking out was a glimmer of brass. He pulled out the bullets lying underneath him. "No, I'm not! Now turn it around!"

The pilot shook his head and then pulled hard right as the balance shifted immediately inside the chopper. "One more pass!"

Thomas loaded the bullets into the feed and wiped the sweat from both eyes. The chopper came back around to view the landing zone. The NVA were swarming. Doc stood as bullets passed through his shoulder and leg. He fell to the ground.

"No, not today, Lord! Not today!" Thomas pulled the trigger and unleashed a barrage of lead into the incoming NVA. He took out dozens. They kept coming. He soon realized he was almost out of bullets. "Drop to head level down there."

The pilot swiveled his head around.

"Not happening!" Thomas grabbed his collar. "You swivel it around now!"

"It's suicide!"

"No, it's a life!"

The pilot swiveled the chopper around and dropped it to a few feet above the ground as the speed of the chopper crossing the field increased.

* * * * *

Doc sat on one knee. He was struggling to breathe. His whole body was burning. It felt like he was being held above a flame. He pulled a knife from his boot as a nearby wounded NVA soldier stumbled to his feet and slowly walked toward him. Everything became silent. Doc watched the soldier's eyes as he pulled a machete from his backside. "Don't you do it." Doc trembled. "Don't, I'm telling you. This isn't worth it."

The NVA soldier talked back to him in a very calm voice, "Come on, man. You don't want to do this." Doc's eyes filled with tears as the NVA soldier stopped within a few feet of Doc. Doc pointed the knife at the soldier. The soldier stared at Doc, then plunged forward at him with the machete. Doc plunged the knife forward as the NVA soldier's machete grazed Doc's cheek. The NVA soldier backed away grasping his side where the knife protruded. He looked up at Doc. Blood dripped from Doc's cheek. He shook as his nerves overwhelmed his emotions. Doc looked around. Smoke filled the air. He couldn't see anything. There was no one else until through the smoke emerged a mass silhouette. Doc's hoped rose as he thought help had finally arrived, but fear gripped him because he was helpless. The silhouette finally emerged as the NVA soldiers swarmed in. Just as fast as he had realized his doom, the smoke cleared for a moment as a shadow passed over his head, and a body rolled in front of him to its feet, barreling toward the incoming NVA.

"Go, my friend," Thomas quickly said as he sprinted into the smoke.

Time slowed down to almost a halt as Doc watched Thomas reach a grenade up to his mouth and pull a pin from a grenade, one in each hand. The NVA soon reached him, stabbing him with their bayonets and firing their handguns into his friend.

"No! Thomas, no!"

Thomas fell to his knees, both hands still gripping the grenades. His grip released the grenades as both fell to the ground. They didn't reach the dirt before the mass of NVA soldiers were dissipated into pieces.

Someone grabbed Doc from behind as he wept for his friend.

"It's going to be okay," they spoke into his ear.

Doc turned to see the young soldier he had found under the bodies earlier dragging him toward the landing zone.

CHAPTER 9

Finding Hope

Doc watched as the trees around him flew by, mountain after mountain. It reminded him a lot of his home. It had been a long trip up from Alabama, but it had taken him several years to build up enough courage to come here and deliver this message. It had weighed heavily on him. Although the war had taken a toll on his heart and mind, Doc was still as optimistic as he always had been, but this was different. He felt so much guilt, and yet there was nothing he could do to make it better. The first few years of being back home had been a battle in itself. Night after sleepless night, all he could think of was Thomas jumping out of that chopper. Doc pulled out the old red-splattered letter that he had held in his front shirt pocket every day since he last saw Thomas. He never lost sight of it. He had prayed and prayed about how to handle this situation, but it seemed like God never answered him on helping build his courage. He feared what Mrs. Bailey would say when she read it. He himself had never even unfolded the old notebook paper. It would have been too painful, and yet it also was not his place to do so. Doc still couldn't figure out if it was his heart or that little piece of paper that weighed him down so much. His thoughts were interrupted as the brakes screeched to a halt. He hadn't noticed the rolling mountains had turned into pavement. "Welcome to Huntington, West Virginia." The bus driver opened the door. Doc gathered his things and headed out.

Doc looked around as younger people walked by in both directions. Most were holding books, and at the end of the street, there sat a majestic-looking statue peering down the street. Doc walked to the end of the street and looked around at the brick buildings. "Marshall University," read a sign in the grass. To the left of the university was a huge facility. Thomas knew he wasn't too far from his destination, but he wasn't quite there. He was just ready to do what he had come to do. He thought maybe one of these students passing might know a way to get where he was heading.

"Ma'am, could you tell me how I may be able to get to Wayne County?" Doc asked a passing woman. The woman ignored Doc and kept walking. "Sir, could you help me?" Doc asked a passing man.

"No, I won't give you any money," the man replied, walking quickly by. Thomas asked a few more passersby, but to no avail. Either nobody knew where Wayne was, or they ignored him. Doc wondered if anybody would help him. He decided to walk across the street to the facility he had seen. He thought maybe the students just weren't from the area, and maybe the people working in this facility were local people who knew their way around.

As Doc walked up to the facility, he saw a group of men laughing and talking. They were all covered in grease from head to toe and smoking cigarettes. As he approached, the men stopped laughing and got quiet.

"Excuse me, gentlemen. I was wondering if any of you might know what direction I could go to get to Wayne?"

The men peered at Doc, blowing smoke and not answering him. One small man toward the back of the group flipped his cigarette on the ground. "What business you got in Wayne?" The small man squinted at Doc.

"Well, I'm looking to deliver a message to someone there." Doc slightly smiled as to be polite.

The small man appeared to be studying Doc's face as he took in his reply. "And who might that someone be?" The small man crossed his arms as if it were up to Doc to explain himself.

"I'm looking for Mrs. Thomas Bailey."

The demeanor of the men standing around changed instantly. Some started toward Doc, but the small man stepped forward to stop them. "What business do you have with her?" A couple men gritted their teeth as Doc took a few paces backward.

"I have something that belongs to her. It was given to me by her husband." Doc pulled out the old folded-up letter. The bloodstains on the letter had turned crimson over time. Doc held up the letter.

"You serve in Nam?" the little man asked, still dryly.

Doc nodded as he slowly placed the letter back into his shirt pocket. The men stepped back as the little man approached Doc. He held his hand out. "Lewis Glenn, Third Calvary."

Doc held out his hand and shook the little man's hand. "They call me Doc. Green Beret."

The small man's eyes filled with tears as a mutual respect was instantly gained. "How can I help you, Doc?"

Doc sat down in the little man's truck as the group of men watched from the distance. "They don't take to strangers very well, do they?" Doc asked as he shut the door.

"Nope, surely don't, especially someone like you looking for Mrs. Bailey."

Doc thought aloud as Lewis started up the truck, "How far away from Wayne are we, Mr. Glenn?"

Glenn rolled down his window and lit another cigarette. "About twenty minutes," Glenn said as he exhaled a cloud of smoke. "You're lucky you found me, buddy. Going into Wayne alone could be a dangerous thing for you."

Doc stared out the window as the concrete street turned into brick laid in the road. "But I'm sure you are no stranger to dangerous situations." Lewis chuckled. "There are a lot of kept-up people around these parts." Doc didn't say anything as Lewis looked over at him a few times to get a reaction. "Well, that letter must be pretty important for you to come all the way out here."

Doc nodded in agreement.

"You see, Mrs. Krauss and that family have been through some rough times since they flooded Stiltner."

Doc looked over at Lewis. "What is Stiltner?"

The small man flipped his cigarette out the window. "I grew up in Stiltner. It was a small town just outside of Wayne. That's where Thomas Bailey grew up also. Back in '63, a huge flood ravaged the town, destroyed everything there. After they build the dam, the whole town was lost to the flood, and it was about that time that Thomas Bailey shipped off to Vietnam. I wasn't far behind him, but I was there to see the impact those events had on the townspeople, especially Emily Krauss."

Doc had never heard this name before. "Emily Krauss?"

"Emily Bailey, I mean. That was her maiden name. Thomas married Emily right before he shipped out. She was pregnant, maybe just a couple months before he left. It's a shame." Lewis shook his head. "That baby was born with a rare condition. That family has struggled. You see, that's why those men were so protective. They are all from the area too. They just don't want to see any bad come to that family. They're good people."

Doc shook his head. Although he had never met the two, deep down, he cared for them just as much as anyone.

"Nobody around here was sure about the circumstances of Thomas's death."

Doc turned his head sharply toward the man.

"We heard he got killed by his own. There was a fella from around these parts who went to boot camp with him. He said Thomas had a hard time of it. He struggled from day one. He was so weak he could barely do push-ups."

"Stop this vehicle." Doc's eyes filled with tears as rage filled his chest.

"Do what?"

"You stop this vehicle right now!"

The man slammed the brakes and pulled off the side of the dusty road. Doc unlatched his seat belt and slid closer to the man. "Let me tell you something." Doc's voice quivered with rage. "I also went through basic with Thomas Bailey, and he was the strongest man I have ever known. So when you see that slimy rat that said that, you tell him he didn't know Thomas Bailey. He didn't know the man I knew." Doc didn't realize he was gripping the man's collar as tightly as he had, then released it. Doc slid back over to his side of the truck and latched his seat belt back.

The man was startled. "That didn't come from me, buddy. I was in a different platoon than you."

"I'm sure you saw some bad things, my friend, but what Thomas Bailey experienced was unimaginable."

The rest of the trip was draped in silence as thoughts of Thomas flashed through Doc's head.

The ride to Wayne was quick as Doc's thoughts of Thomas made his nerves go away.

"We're here, buddy," the little man said as he pulled up into a gravel driveway.

Doc looked around at the little houses in the neighborhood. Most were in bad condition. The siding was coming off the little yellow house in front of them, and part of the gutter had fallen from the roof. The two men walked up the little set of steps onto the porch and stood in front of the old beat-up stained pine door. The little man knocked a few times. Doc's heart was beating out of his chest. His palms were sweating as he gripped the bloodstained note inside his clenched fist. Out of the corner of his eye, he saw a little pair of eyes peering out of the window at him. As he looked into the little eyes, the front door opened abruptly. A beautiful young woman stood in the doorway. "Can I help you?" A man stood closely behind her. He was older, but stood closely, looking sternly at the two men.

"Ms. Bailey, I apologize for bothering you, but I happened to run across this fella, and he said he has something that belonged to your husband and wanted to give it to you."

Doc noticed the woman look over and look at him up and down. She stepped back and slammed the door. The little man pursed his lips and looked up at Doc. "I didn't figure this would go too well." The little man knocked again. "Ms. Krauss, please give this man a chance to explain." The two men waited for a couple minutes, but nobody came back to the door.

Doc was hurt that he couldn't explain what happened to Thomas to his family. He had waited and thought so long and so hard about this and made the journey all this way just to come up short. The little man had started to walk off the porch when Doc stepped up to the door. He was torn because he didn't want to cause the family any more pain, but his heart weighed heavy as he spoke through the door softly. "Ma'am, I served with your husband throughout most of the war. He gave me something he wanted you to have. He told me to give it to you." Doc waited a few seconds, but to no avail. "I'm just going to leave it right here inside your door, and I'll leave." Doc bent down and started to slip the letter in the door when it cracked open slightly. Doc looked up and saw the little pair of eyes looking down at him.

"Did you know my daddy?"

Tears filled Doc's eyes as he looked at the little girl. "Yes, I knew him well."

The door opened more as the woman stood closely behind her. "Grace, go back to your room for a minute. I need to talk to this man alone. Can you do that for mommy?" Emily bent down and brushed the little girl's hair out from in front of her eyes.

"Yes, Momma." The little girl scurried back through the hall-way and out of sight as Emily opened the door and came out onto the porch and shut the door behind her.

"Have a seat," Emily said as she nodded toward the two rocking chairs that sat on the porch.

"Yes, ma'am." Doc sat down in the old white rocking chair, as did Emily in the other.

"I don't believe you told me what your name is, Mr...."

"Mr. Washington, but everyone calls me Doc."

Emily sat up in her chair. "What is it that my husband wanted me to have?"

Doc opened his palm and looked at the letter Thomas had given him. This letter had been with Doc since the moment of Thomas's death, and it had survived Vietnam and through the dark years of Doc's life transitioning back into his regular life. He had wept many nights over this letter and had guarded it with his own life to get it to this point and this moment. Doc swallowed and reached out his hand. Emily slowly reached hers out to retrieve the letter.

"Ma'am"—tears streamed down Doc's face—"this letter was given to me before your husband died. He gave me this letter and told me no matter what happens, get this to my wife. He made me promise."

Emily felt the letter's weight as she clutched it in her hands. She looked at it sitting in her palm. The bloodstains splattered across the paper made Emily tremble. "Well, thank you for bringing it to me," Emily said quickly as she stood up from out of the chair. "If you'll excuse me, I have business to attend to." The pain was unbearable to her. There had been no closure as the events surrounding Thomas's death had never been explained. Emily turned to go back into the house as Doc stood up.

"Ma'am, I just wanted you to know that your husband was a hero. He died—" Doc struggled to pull what he had wanted to say all this time deep from within himself. "He died giving his life so that other good men could live."

Emily turned back to face him. "I've always known my husband was a good man. No matter what anyone else has said."

Doc slowly nodded. "He was my friend," Doc said. "He was my only friend in that hell." He wiped the tears from his face. "Are you religious, ma'am?" Doc didn't hesitate. "Well, whether you are or are not, your husband and I developed a strong relationship and had many conversations about God while we were over there. We saw so many things that would make you question if there truly was a God, and if so, why is he letting these types of things happen? To women and children? But through it all, your husband came to believe that God was not only real that but he had been sent there to Vietnam for a purpose by God. Now, I don't know what that purpose was, but he believed so deeply that it also made me believe the same. Your husband became a follower of Christ in that place over there, and for the past five years, I have struggled to understand how a man could love Christ and keep him inside him living through all that we did and saw over there. I've also struggled with hatred—toward not only myself but also toward God. As I lie down to sleep every night, I see your husband's face. I play through those last few moments over and over again and wonder why was it not me that died instead of him? I wished it was me. Every second—and I don't understand everything that happened and why—but when I think back to what he told me, I somehow pull myself out of that dark hole I keep on finding myself in. I'll never forget those words he said: *For by grace are you saved.* I thought I knew the Lord long before I heard your husband say this to me, but I've had to dig within myself to find out who I truly am." Doc shook his head. "Through grace, we are saved."

Doc and Emily stood there in silence, both staring at the porch. Both were thinking about Thomas. Both were still confused and searching for what seemed like impossible answers.

Emily sat back down in the old white rocking chair. Doc stood looking out at the mountains that surrounded the small community. "Is the place Thomas grew up close to here?" he asked.

Emily nodded as she stared at the letter still in her hands.

"Do you think it would be all right if I went to see it?"

Emily's attention returned to Doc. "There's nothing left to see. It is all gone."

"Even his old cabin?"

Emily was slightly taken aback by Doc's question. Thomas must have been very close to this man to tell him about his old home. "Yes, It's just a pile of rubble."

Doc turned back to Emily. "I've waited many years to come here and try to find some type of closure to all this. I feel that if I can see something good about Thomas's life, I could find some way of drowning out"—Doc cut his sentence short; he didn't want to go into detail about that final day—"some way of remembering the good."

Emily took a deep breath. "I don't think I could stand it." She placed her hands in her face as tears began to fall down her cheeks. "We lost everything there. Sometimes I feel that Thomas is still back there, and all of my memories with him."

Doc swallowed a dry gulp.

"I'll take you."

The stern voice startled both Doc and Emily. Doc turned to see the man who was behind Emily earlier.

"Daddy, you don't have to—"

"Yes, I do. It's been put on my heart to help this man." Mr. Krauss fiddled with his old cap. "We'll go first thing in the morning. You can help me get the boat ready tonight and sleep here."

Doc smiled slightly. "Thank you, sir."

Doc and Mr. Krauss woke up early and headed out the winding road out of town. It was a foggy morning. Mr. Krauss's hair had started to turn gray, and his eyes were wrinkled as the stresses of his internal battles were starting to show outwardly. Doc watched as they would pass by a small house once in a while on the curvy road.

"It's been a very hard time for my daughter over the past few years."

Doc listened as his exhaustion from his trip had not worn off yet.

"When Thomas left, the reality of the situation had not set in for Emily. Of course, we knew it was a possibility that Thomas wouldn't come home, but losing her mother on top of Thomas and Grace's illness was a lot for her to bear. We lost our house…we lost everything." Mr. Krauss tapped his thumb against the steering wheel. "So you knew Thomas well?"

Doc nodded. "Yes, sir, I did. We were good friends through a lot of bad times."

There was silence until Mr. Krauss abruptly asked, "Did he die in vain?"

Doc hadn't thought much about the events surrounding Thomas's death, but this made him realize that not only did nobody know of the events surrounding Thomas's death but that he was not the only one without closure. This bothered Doc a lot. Thomas was a hero. Not even his family knew about Thomas's actions.

"Thomas was the bravest man I've ever known, sir." Doc still wasn't ready to replay those moments in his head as he had tried his best to forget them. He found himself at a loss for words. The silence was comfortable in this situation.

"That eases some pain I've felt for years."

The rest of the drive was quiet.

The two men pulled up to the boat ramp where a newly painted sign was posted onto two old railroad ties: "East Lynn Lake." Doc and

Mr. Krauss unloaded the old stainless steel boat and placed the rutter into the water. Doc looked around at how majestic the surrounding mountains rolled into the dark water and reflected the mood of the trees. The fog sat a few feet from the surface and created an almost undiscovered scene as if nobody had ever seen what the two men were experiencing.

"Under this water sits a road that led into town. It curved around that bend up ahead." Mr. Krauss motioned with his hand toward the water's curve, and the little boat pushed slowly through the water. As they rounded the turn, there sat an open part of the lake that was much wider. "That was where our little town sat. There was a post office there, and the Mills'/ Vaughn Store sat back in that corner."

Doc looked around as he envisioned what the buildings must have looked like. As his eyes passed over the hills, he noticed a small white building sitting well out of the water overlooking the scene. "What is that?" Doc asked as he pointed.

"That's the old church." Mr. Krauss's head hung looking toward his feet as the engine's motor came to a purr.

Doc turned around and saw that Mr. Krauss was visibly shaken up. "Sir, are you all right?"

Mr. Krauss wiped the falling tears from his face and snuffed his nose. "Yeah, I'm all right. There are just a lot of memories in that old building. That's where Emily and Thomas were married."

Doc turned back around and took in every inch of the old church. He thought of how much Thomas had loved Emily. It was intertwined with every sentence he used to speak of her. He thought of how beautiful Emily must have been and how happy Thomas must have felt.

"I want to show you something else." Mr. Krauss pressed down on the gas of the little trolling motor and turned the boat toward a small cove toward the back of the opening in the lake.

As the two men reached the opening, Doc could see that a small creek led up through the hollow. At the top of this mountain sat three crosses. They overlooked the body of water majestically. It was as if they were the only sign of human life to ever see this place. The scene was one of the most beautiful Doc had ever seen. A willow tree reached out over the water and kissed the surface while the breeze blew and slightly shook the branches as if it were welcoming the two men. Birds chirped, and Doc could see fish swimming slowly through the clear and shallow water. Two deer drank from the creek bank ahead, and the fog had lifted as the sun shone sharply through the branches to crystallize the still current of the water. Doc was transfixed in a moment of serenity. It was as if this place spoke to him through Thomas's lasting spirit. "Beautiful, isn't it?"

Doc nodded. He didn't want to say a word as his heart was filled with a presence he hadn't felt in many years.

"Thomas was the one who placed those crosses on the hillside. He carved them out of an old tree on that hillside. He believed it was the tree that was struck by lightning the night his mother had an accident. She wasn't right after that night."

Doc and Mr. Krauss made their way all the way up the creek until the boat was too wide to go any farther. "Help me pull this boat up." The water flowed from a small runoff flowing from down the hillside. There beside it was a small path. The two men walked up the path; Mr. Krauss led the way, followed closely by Doc. After walking up the steep mountain, the two men made it to a clearing that sat on a point on the mountain. There in the middle, the weeds had grown up around the stone that had once been the old cabin where Thomas had lived.

"That's what's left of where Thomas grew up."

Doc walked over to the torched wood. Moss had started to creep up the old stones that stood stacked up. Doc stepped into the singed square within the weeds and looked around. As he studied the surroundings, Doc closed his eyes and began to hear Thomas's words play through his head: *I used to sit at that old pine table and just stare at the flame. I wondered if I would ever feel something inside me I once had as a boy. Over time, I lost it. The day I fell in love with Emily, something sparked that flame again, and I could feel again. My heart had life again.*

Doc opened his eyes and walked back over to Mr. Krauss. As he passed over the charred remains, his foot hit something sticking out of the ground. Doc looked down as a small black box had become visible. Doc bent down and picked up the small charred box. He swept off the debris that covered it and blew the dust off the keyhole.

"I wonder what that is?" Mr. Krauss asked.

"I'm not sure, but I know Emily may like to have it. There may be something of Thomas's inside it."

"I'd say there probably isn't much in it, but it'd do us well to take it."

The two looked around a bit more and soon headed back over the hill to the little boat and made their way back down the lake toward the boat ramp. It was a lot for Doc to take in, but it made him a little more at ease putting some memories to rest and pictures with stories that Thomas had told him.

The two arrived back at the old house in Wayne to find Emily sitting and waiting on the porch. She was there to greet her father at the bottom of the stairs, holding Grace. "How was the trip?" Emily had a stern tone to her voice.

"It was good, sweetie. It brought back a lot of good memories."

"Did you find what you were looking for?" Emily asked Doc.

"It helped me piece some things together," he said, nodding his head. "Oh, I almost forgot that we found something at the house seat." Doc pulled out the charred box.

"Thomas's cabin? I didn't think there was anything left."

"There wasn't, except for this," Doc said as he handed her the box.

She grasped the box and looked it over. "What's in it?"

"We're not sure. We couldn't get it open."

Emily took the box and sat it on the hood of her father's truck. She wondered what it could be.

"Mama," Grace interrupted.

"Hold on, baby, we're trying to figure something out."

Emily, Doc, and Mr. Krauss looked the box over, trying to find a way to open it. It was sealed tightly and was very heavy, which made it nearly impossible to bust open.

"Mama—"

"Hold on, sweetie."

"Mama, why don't you use your key?"

Emily stopped what she was doing and looked at Grace. She was pointing to the necklace that Emily found in Thomas's jeans pocket the day he had left for the army. "Sweetie, I don't think that key belongs to this."

"Well, why don't you just try, Mommy?"

Emily smiled and nodded. She pulled out the old key and picked up the box and slid it in the keyhole. The box popped open as she twisted. Emily gasped.

"Well, my word." Mr. Krauss chuckled as he came closer to look at the box.

Emily opened the lid and reached inside. Her fingertips slid over a group of photos. Emily pulled them out, looking at each one closely. They were of Thomas as a child. Emily began to weep as she fumbled through the pictures. She wrapped her arms around her father.

"She didn't have any pictures of him," Mr. Krauss quietly told Doc.

Doc nodded and smiled slightly. "Well, now she does."

The four headed inside. Doc started to follow when he noticed Emily had left the box lying on the hood. He picked up the box and started to shut the lid when he noticed a glimmer shine from inside the box. He reached down and pulled out a key. He examined it closely. Doc could tell it was a key to an automobile. He flipped it over and tried to wipe the rust away. There, on the other side, he noticed an emblem. "Plymouth." Doc stuck the key in his pocket and headed inside.

CHAPTER 10

Mysterious Ways

Emily sat on the couch and fumbled through the pictures. Tears rolled down her cheeks as the photos of Thomas brought back so many memories. She saw a lot of him in Grace. As the memories came flooding back into her mind, she cherished the short time she had spent with him. Doc sat and stared down at the key he had found in the old rusty box. His curiosity had him intrigued on not only the pictures but also why this key was in this box. "Did Thomas have a car?"

Emily looked up as her attention was still on the old pictures. "No, he didn't," she replied.

Doc stared intently on the key. "That's strange," Doc said softly. "Then I wonder whose key this is?" Doc held the key up for Emily to see.

Mr. Krauss got up from his seat and sat down next to Doc. "That's an old Plymouth key, it looks like." Mr. Krauss took the key and looked it over. "That's to an older-model car."

Emily's attention was now on the key as the two men studied it intently. "Where did you find that key, Doc?" Emily asked.

"Inside the bottom of that box we found."

Emily got up and went over to look at the key. "Let me see it."

Mr. Krauss handed her the key, and she held it up to the light. "You said this was to a Plymouth?" Emily asked. She put the key down to her side and stared away from the men.

Mr. Krauss looked at Doc and back to his daughter. "Yes, it is," Mr. Krauss answered.

Emily was silent for a moment, and then she looked back down at the key. "I know what car this key goes to." She looked up at her father.

The four piled into the old rusty station wagon and pulled out of the gravel driveway. Night had come and gone, and not one of the adults had slept a wink. Doc was too curious as to what was happening. Emily hadn't explained herself the night before. She had told them that she knew what vehicle the key belonged to and then walked back into the hallway, only to return the following morning holding both the letter and the key, one in each hand. Doc had noticed that the letter was now opened up, and Emily's face bore a different look since he had met her. She seemed relieved in some strange way. Doc had thought many sleepless nights of opening that letter, but he dared not dishonor his commitment to his loyal friend to return it to its rightful owner. He had accomplished that and fought many internal battles in doing so. To see this look on Emily's face made Doc wonder if what that letter held could also give him some sort of peace. But as much as he wanted to feel at peace about what Thomas had done, he felt better knowing he had done the right thing. Somehow he had thought that coming up to West Virginia and delivering this letter would ease his internal suffering, but it seemed like now there were more questions than answers.

This place left a man wondering about not only life but his identity. It was mysterious in the fact that time seemed to stop, and he was caught in something that left him uneasy. All these thoughts and feelings played well into the scenery of the sun peeking through the top of the surrounding mountains as they passed through the hills and headed back toward the lake where Mr. Krauss had showed him the place that was once their home. He was along for this confusing ride no matter what the outcome would be, but he questioned whether there would even be an outcome. There hadn't been much said between Emily and him or Mr. Krauss. She just asked that Mr. Krauss take her to the lake and asked that Doc come with them.

As they pulled into the marina, the sun was now hidden beneath the darkness of clouds, and the breeze slightly whipped Emily's beautiful hair to the side of her face as she looked out over the water. Mr. Krauss held Grace's hand, and Doc stood closely by curiously watching Emily.

"Sir, is she all right?" Doc asked Mr. Krauss. Doc pursed his lips and looked down at Grace.

"I think she'll be all right. You see, this is the first time she has been back here since they flooded the town."

Doc nodded and turned his attention back to the dark clouds that were slowly blowing in from the north. "Looks like there might be a storm blowing in," Doc said as he looked for a reaction from Emily.

Emily stared intently at the mountains as if she were in another place. Her eyes were glassy, and Doc could see the effect this place had on her. Her silence was broken, though her eyes never left the horizon. "I want to go to the old homeplace."

Doc looked at Mr. Krauss as the wind picked up around them. "Emily, it's about to storm—"

"I want to go to the old homeplace." Emily turned to face Doc and Mr. Krauss.

Doc looked past her to the far hillside. A blanket of rain was falling heavily in the distance and was steadily making its way toward them. Doc looked to Mr. Krauss and down at Grace. Her little eyes looked up at him with a shine. "I'll go with you," Doc said as he looked at Mr. Krauss for approval.

"I'm not sure, Doc. I mean, you don't know your way around, and if you get lost, you will have trouble if anyone sees you with—"

"He can come with me," Emily interrupted him.

Mr. Krauss looked at Emily. He could tell by her face that there was no convincing her otherwise. "Okay, we will wait here in the car for you." Doc and Emily pulled the old small johnboat out of the back of the truck and got the boat in the water just as the rain soaked them down.

Doc steered the boat as Emily looked ahead through the downpour of rain. The visibility was low, and Doc had no idea where they were on the lake. Emily navigated around each bend in the lake as every corner looked just like the last to Doc. He was soaked to the bone, but the warm summer air kept him from chilling. Emily's hair ran down her back, and water dripped off her porcelain face, but her eyes shone as brightly in the rain as they did the sun. After passing bend after bend, Emily pointed to the bank. "Go right there."

Doc turned the motor and headed into the bank that lay at the steepest hillside he had seen around the bend. To him, every mountain looked similar, but this one looked to be straight up and down. As he pulled the boat in and tied it off to a tree, he noticed a small path that had grown up with weeds leading up the hillside.

"This is the way," Emily said as she started up the path into the forest.

As Doc followed not far behind, he couldn't help but wonder where they were headed. "Where are we headed, if you don't mind me asking?"

"To try and find what we both have been searching for," Emily answered as she trenched up the muddy hillside.

Doc stopped as Emily's feet slid up the muddy mountain. She fought every step as she slid and fell many times, just trying to get where she was eagerly going. She had caught Doc's attention with her reply, and he too was fighting through the mud and leaves, just trying to make it where Emily was leading him. Soon Doc could see the top of the mountain ahead. Daylight brightened the forest, and Emily reached the top as Doc was not far behind. The top of the mountain was covered with a pine thicket. The brown needles covered the ground, and the light had disappeared from the thick branches that blanketed it. Emily walked into the thicket, and Doc followed.

As they walked through the trees, Thomas looked ahead and saw a clearing in the thicket. The sound of the rain had changed as the trees gave way to the view of an old car looking out over the lake. Emily was standing there beside it, both of her hands on the window as she peered into the old Plymouth. Doc stood in amazement at the queer scene. It was such an impossible sight in an unbelievable place at the top of this seemingly lonely mountain.

Doc walked over to the old car, which was covered in pine needles. "This is unbelievable," Doc whispered as he looked out across the lake. There sitting not far from the car were the three crosses he had seen just the day before. When he realized where he was, the visions of the once-buzzing town of Stiltner flashed through his imagination. He heard Mr. Krauss's voice describe the buildings and streets, and he looked down from the hidden wonder that lay at the top of this mountain.

"This is a very special place to me," Emily said as she looked out at the crosses.

Doc could hear the emotion pouring from her words. He looked over to her. Although her face was dripping from the rain, Doc could see the tears blending into the raindrops.

"This was a very special place to Thomas, more so than anybody," she said as she wiped her hair away from her eyes. Mud smeared over her cheeks and forehead as she stood shivering under the pines. "Thomas would come here to get away from everything. It was a very private place to him. Matter of fact, I believe you are just the second person besides myself to know of this place."

Doc nodded. He remembered Thomas describe such a place to him one night as they sat together in a muddy hole in the jungle. The rain had reminded him of a time he spent with Emily, and he told Doc about the special nights he spent with Emily in the very place he was now standing.

"Thomas said you were a good friend to him," Emily changed the subject.

Doc nodded. "He was my friend."

"Do you still have that key on you?"

Doc had forgotten about the key. The shock of the situation had taken his attention off the fact that the key in his pocket went to this old car. "Yes." Doc fumbled through his pockets and found the old key. He pulled it out and handed it over to Emily. She placed the key into the lock and turned. The lock popped up as she looked over to Doc. "Well, I'll be...," Doc said as he smiled.

Emily got into the car and unlocked the passenger's side. "Come in and have a seat."

Doc climbed in and sat down. The rain tapped against the glass as the scene of the lake was blurred by the falling rain. Emily looked out of the windshield. "I read the letter you brought to me."

Doc turned to Emily.

Emily smiled slightly. "Thomas was always a good man. His heart was just torn because he felt nobody loved him."

"I know he was," Doc said quietly but confidently. "He said in his letter that, as he passed on, to not dwell on it but rather to be happy and have peace, knowing he was in a better place. He said I needed to try and strengthen my relationship with God because that is what healed him. He said that true treasure lies at the foot of the cross. I'm still not sure what that means, but I know someday I will." Doc sat silently, listening intently, searching for anything that would put his mind at ease. Although those words helped, the guilt still seemed to soak his heart.

"I just wish he could be here to see his daughter. I thought I wouldn't make it after I found out he had passed away. I wasn't sure what kind of mother I would be. Grace's condition...," Emily hesitated. "Grace's condition doesn't give her much time. I just wish that Thomas could be here. Maybe things would be easier on us."

Doc sat and listened while his heart swelled with every word. "There is something I need to tell you, ma'am." Doc placed his hands together, and his nerves tied his stomach into a knot. His heart couldn't take the guilt anymore. He had to tell Emily the truth. "Ma'am, your husband...he gave his life to save my own."

Emily looked over to Doc.

"It's been weighing on me for a very long time. It was Thomas's last mission. He didn't even get sent out with us that day. They let him ride in the chopper to pick us up." Doc stopped as he shook his head. "It was supposed to be a routine patrol to check. The report said there was no Vietcong in the area. We left early in the morning. Thomas stayed back on the colonel's orders. He had been through so many missions already. He was lucky to be alive. We left out before dawn, patrolled all day long, and never saw a thing. We got back to the landing zone, the chopper came down, and I was the last man to board. As the first few men boarded the chopper, an entire group of Vietcong came out from beneath us. They ambushed us…killed almost everybody. I ran for the chopper, and they were all over me. I got hit in the back. It knocked me down. As I looked behind me, I saw a few guys jump out of the chopper. When they got to me, I could see your husband was one of them. But he didn't stop. He kept on running forward. The other two men dragged me back to the chopper as I watched at least thirty Vietcong swarm incoming toward the helicopter."

Doc stopped and tried to swallow as the memories stuck like a knife in his chest. Tears rolled down his cheeks as he thought of those last few moments of Thomas's life. "Your husband shot at least fifteen before he ran out of bullets. He pulled two grenades as they overran him. I tried my best to get back to him, but they held me down." Doc took a deep breath. He sat in silence as he tried to find something to say, but there were no words that could comfort either of them. "I wish every day it was me, ma'am. I truly do."

Emily sat taking in the story. "So my husband died to save your life," Emily said as her voice quivered."

Doc nodded slightly, and he finally got the breath to answer her. "Yes, ma'am, he did."

Emily wiped her eyes. "Well, you must have been a special person to him," she said dryly as she opened the car door.

"Ma'am." Doc opened up his car door and stepped out onto the pine needles.

Emily walked back down the path from where they had come from. "I should have never come here. I'm not sure why he asked me to bring you here."

Doc started to walk after Emily. He understood her anger but felt terrible about the situation. "Ma'am, I'm sorry."

Emily stopped and fell onto the soft soil. Pain overwhelmed her as she wept uncontrollably. Doc walked over and hesitantly bent down. He placed his hand on her back, and she screamed in heartache.

The rain pattering on the leaves echoed through Doc's ears as he sat by Emily in the mud. Doc's mind was numb. He sat back and looked up at the sky and closed his eyes. He thought of nothing as the raindrops hit his face. "Thomas told me once that life wasn't about living in peace but loving in the chaos. He said that as we had bullets flying past our ears." Doc chuckled a little. Emily's sobs softened. "He said, 'You know, Doc, God works in mysterious ways. He will give you hell when you want heaven just to see if heaven is really what you want. And if heaven is what you choose, you will find it at the foot of the cross.'" Doc got up off the ground and looked back into the pine thicket. He walked back into the woods as Emily looked up to see him walking away.

"Where are you going?"

Doc kept walking quickly. "To the foot of the cross."

Emily got up off the ground as Doc disappeared out of sight. She made her way through the thicket and made it to the clearing to see Doc standing at the foot of the middle cross holding something in his hands. As he turned to her, smiling, she was blinded by a flash. The noise was deafening as the ring in her ears was excruciating. She was dizzy and could feel the rain hitting her forehead as she opened her eyes. She looked at the sky, trying to remember what had happened. She remembered she was on the mountain with Doc, and she had run to the cross. Then she saw a flash and woke up lying on the ground. Emily moved her head left and saw the crosses standing tall. It took a moment to register that the gold cross was smoking from the top main beam. As her eyes made their way down the cross, she noticed smoke rolling out of the ground from the cross all the way to her feet. Roots protruded out of the ground, and fresh soil lay pushed up from the earth around the smoking roots. There in the soil lay Doc on his back. Smoke rose from his feet as he lay motionless on the ground. Emily got up slowly, stumbling over her feet, which were tingling. She walked clumsily over to Doc, tripping on each root she met. Doc lay motionless. His eyes were open as the rain fell on his face.

"Doc!" Emily clumsily made her way over to him. "Are you okay!"

Doc stared into the sky as smoke rolled from beneath him crawling up from holes in the ground. He lifted his neck from off the ground and looked at Emily for a second and lay his head back down. "Ma'am." Doc paused. "I believe I know the reason I came here."

Emily fell by Doc's side and grasped his hand. She was in shock and had no words for what had just happened. "I've got a message for you from the Lord. It is time to let go of your grudges." Doc struggled to get the words out.

"It is time to get rid of your anger and your hatred against God. He loves you, no matter the circumstances, and he wants you to give your life to him. He wants me to do the same. Know you are loved, and know that Thomas loved you as well." Doc squeezed Emily's hand. "You know, I never thought I'd end up here at this place, in this moment, but somehow I know this is where I'm supposed to be. I want you to know that Thomas gave his life to the Lord shortly before he died. It's no coincidence that I'm here right now with you. I've seen your bitterness, and Thomas had the same thing inside him when I met him, but he let it go. If he can do it, so can you. I know he would want that for you." Doc turned his eyes back to the sky and gasped for a breath.

Emily started to cry as the rain poured down on Doc's face. "I don't understand all this. Why?"

Doc blinked and looked at Emily. "There is always a bigger plan, Emily. There is always a greater purpose, even if it's hidden under the surface of what things appear to be." Doc then grabbed Emily's arm, and released the item he had retrieved into her hand.

Emily held Doc as he struggled to breath. His breaths became shorter, and soon the tension of his grip on Emily's hand released. Doc was gone.

Emily sat beneath the crosses and watched as the water slowly trickled through the streets below. Her heart was unbearably heavy. There below her, the crumbled cinderblock and gravel streets were captured in a frozen moment of what used to be. The breeze blew through the new greenery that the spring season had birthed. It reminded Emily of the last days she spent with Thomas before the flood. The raindrops fell on Emily's soft face as the thunder rumbled in the distance. Losing almost everything she had ever known was surreal, but seeing the one thing left from her past struck her with a sense of irony. She thought back to Thomas and the light he had shed on the town in that dire time of need when all hope seemed lost. The town may be soon drowned out of sight, but the crosses Thomas's hands bore stood firmly at the hilltop, looking out over the sleepy town that he had given hope. Emily stood up and proudly looked back at what was left of Thomas's memory.

In the weeks and months that followed, Doc's body was sent back home. He was buried in his hometown where he received full military honors. The dam was constructed in East Lynn, and the rains soon filled the streets with water, and then the buildings' roofs soon followed. Many people moved to surrounding towns and hollows. The town became a memory sealed beneath its murky waters.

CHAPTER 11

The Greater Good—Conclusion

Mr. Avery mowed the grass at the new cemetery and upkept the crosses by the lake until his death nearly fifteen years after Stiltner was flooded. He went and saw Grace every Sunday and told her stories about her father until the very end. He was buried in East Lynn, WV in the same cemetery he helped move and establish.

Emily Bailey raised Grace in the nearby town of Wayne, West Virginia. She remarried some years later and, to the day of her death, went and visited the old car on the hill every anniversary of her and Thomas's marriage. She was there the day they brought him home, with the letter clenched tightly in her palm that Doc had delivered in one hand, and the item from the foot of the cross in the other. She was baptized in the lake soon after Doc's death, the crosses overlooking her as she came out of the water a new woman. Emily went on to find a new church and was a Sunday school teacher until her death some years later.

Grace Bailey went on to become a schoolteacher and a Christian missionary. Her proudest moment was when she was escorted to Vietnam to retrieve her father's remains. She was brought home with her father and went on to help disabled Vietnam veterans dealing with depression and visited those suffering from the effects of Agent Orange in Vietnam.

After Thomas Bailey's death, his property was sold to the local government. The property was excavated, and underneath the house seat lay a chest with approximately $80,000. A note was found inside, reading, "Blessed are the poor in Spirit." It was signed by Thomas's mother. The money was given to Grace, who in turn gave it to Doc's family. They erected a boys' home in Florida named in his honor.

ABOUT THE AUTHOR

Cody K. Mills is a United States Navy veteran who served on board a guided missile destroyer during the War on Terror. He grew up in rural West Virginia, and his world travels and interactions with various cultures and peoples inspired him to become an author to tell the true stories of his lessons and experiences learned. He has lived across the United States and now resides back in his home town in West Virginia with his wife and four children. He is a homesteader and enjoys farming, coaching sports, and living a simple life with his family.

CPSIA information can be obtained
at www.ICGtesting.com
Printed in the USA
LVHW030341020221
678105LV00006B/159

9 781098 057510